# How To Swallow A Pig

## LEGAL NOTICE

The phrase "spoken word poetry" is copyright Poetryco and may not be used hereafter without written consent. Any such use is subject to a licensing fee and/or fine. Also, the words "spoken," "word," and "poetry" are each trademarks of Poetryco, as are all of their separated phonemes. So-called promotion agents of bars, clubs, concerts, and venues of all kinds, including radio, are hereby ordered to discontinue use of these words in their advertising and promotional material both separately and in context. The issue of ownership of the brand names "Performance Poet" and "Performance Artist" is currently before the courts, but all users of these phrases should be advised that in the event Poetryco, as expected, wins its suit, all users are being tracked and at such time will be subject to licensing fees plus any accrued interest. The logos "Beat Poet" and "Language Poet" are temporarily retired from service and are not to be used under any circumstances until they are redefined by Poetryco's board of directors.

Poetryco is a "for-profit" company.

Please consult Poetryco's free on-line index for information on our copyrights of the following words and names: "Literature," "Racist," "Freedom," "Terror," "Billie," and "McDonald."

---

Poetryco: the company that brings you the trusted Poem Brand. Making sure that language is safe, controllable *and* affordable, since 1984.

Robert Priest
# How To Swallow A Pig

ECW PRESS
MISFIT

Copyright © Robert Priest, 2004

Published by ECW PRESS
2120 Queen Street East, Suite 200, Toronto, Ontario, Canada M4E 1E2

All rights reserved. No part of this publication may be reproduced, stored in a retrieval system, or transmitted in any form by any process — electronic, mechanical, photocopying, recording, or otherwise — without the prior written permission of the copyright owners and ECW PRESS.

NATIONAL LIBRARY OF CANADA CATALOGUING IN PUBLICATION

Priest, Robert, 1951–
How to swallow a pig / Robert Priest.

ISBN 1-55022-649-5
I. Title.
PS8581.R47H69 2004     C818'.5407     C2004-902603-8

Editor: Michael Holmes/a misFit book
Cover and Text Design: Darren Holmes
Author Photo: Robert Priest
Production and Typesetting: Mary Bowness
Printing: Marc Veilleux Imprimeur

This book is set in Goudy.

The publication of *How To Swallow a Pig* has been generously supported by the Canada Council, the Ontario Arts Council, the Ontario Media Development Corporation, and the Government of Canada through the Book Publishing Industry Development Program. **Canadä**

DISTRIBUTION
CANADA: Jaguar Book Group, 100 Armstrong Avenue, Georgetown, ON, L7G 5S4

PRINTED AND BOUND IN CANADA

To my beloved, Marsha Kirzner

## ACKNOWLEDGEMENTS

Over the past 30 years, my prose poems have appeared in numerous publications, including the following books: *Sadness of Spacemen* (Dreadnaught Press, 1980), *The Man Who Broke Out of the Letter X* (Coach House Press, 1984), *The Mad Hand* (Coach House Press, 1988), *Scream Blue Living* (The Mercury Press, 1992) and *Resurrection in the Cartoon* (ECW Press, 1997). Some have also been broadcast on the CBC.

Thanks to the editors of those books: Albert Moritz, Linda Davey, Christopher Dewdney, Bev Daurio, and Michael Holmes.

The author also gratefully acknowledges the financial assistance of The Canada Council for the Arts, The Ontario Arts Council, The Toronto Arts Council, and the George Woodcock Fund.

Thanks also to Mendelson Joe, John Lennon, Lillian Allen, Allen Booth, Marsha Kirzner, Eleanor Kirzner, Eleanor Cruise, my parents, my brother and sister — and to my children.

Some of these poems are available as videos online at www.poempainter.com

*How to Swallow a Pig* is Volume 2 of *Phormacopia*. Volume 1, *Blue Pyramids: New and Selected Poems* is also available from ECW Press.

# CONTENT

## BOOK 1
## VENTRILOQUISM FOR DUMMIES

How to Swallow a Pig   3
Instructions for Laughter   5
Colours of Bullshit   6
Peaches   7
Mangoes   8
Sweet and Sour Angel Wings   9
Secrets of Paper   10
Paper   11
The School Behind the School   12
Substitute Tag: An Idea for a Children's Game   13
Eggshell Children   14
How to Visit Me on My Cliff Top   15
Textual Difficulties   16
How to Catch a Deity   18
The Cup of Words   19
Ink   20

## BOOK 2
## FROM THE INTERSTELLAR LIBRARY ON ARCTURUS

The Early Education of the Num-nums   23
Falling in Hate   24
The Arms Race of Obbagga   25
Beautiful Money   26
The Zelgs   27
Psanthosians   29
Report on the Earth-Air Addicts   30
The Environmental Leap Forward   31
Sadness of Spacemen   33

## BOOK 3
## ADVENTURES OF MY HAND

Candles   37
The Retroactive Orphan   38
The Ancestry   39
My Huge Voice   41
Halters   42
In Stupid School   44
On the Assembly Line   45
At the Doctor of Flaws   46
Adventures of My Hand   48
My Therapeutic Cock   49
Precautionary Chandeliers   50
Silence is Coming   51
All the Sounds a Scared Man Hears   52
Jack the Insomniac   53
Portrait of the Artist   55

# BOOK 4
# UNSTABLE FABLES

Lives of Dah   59
The Unfortunate Genius and His "Winkle"   60
The Vanishing Brassiere   63
His Little Mother   66
Little Hurts   67
Textual Pleasure   68
Fable of a Fable   70
Birth of a Tree   71
The Misuse of Cradles   73
The Little Singer   74
A Very Leaky Faucet   75
The Pig Who Discovered Happiness   76
The Little Pig of Self-respect   77
The Violent Man's Hand   78
The Mad Hand   79
The Escaped Cock   81
The Man with the Nitroglycerin Tears   82
The Man Who Broke Out of the Letter X   84
The Wise Man   85
Points   87
The Man Who Thought a Woman Was God   88
The Uncatchable Man   90
Poet's Progress   92
Hit Songs from Heaven   93
Sultan of the Snowflakes   94
Ego-angels   95
Quiet Caps   96
Want the Water!   97

# BOOK 5
# COMIX

CURLY'S REPORT   101
WITNESS REPORT   102
WITNESS REPORT II   103
THE STOOGE BY-LAWS
THE THREE DISCIPLE STOOGES   104
MY THREE STOOGES   106
THE THREE SEXUAL SURVIVOR STOOGES   107
BLADERUNNER STOOGES   108
THE IMMORTAL STOOGES   109
CURLY, LARRY, AND OSWALD   110
THE PRESLEY TWINS   111
PARALLELVIS UNIVERSE 2003   113
THE NEW CRUISE MAN   114
THE COMBINATION CRUISE MAN AND WOMAN   115
THE SURREALIST AIR FORCE   116
ORDNANCE IN SODOM   118
WMDS   119
THE EXECUTION OF MALNUTRITION   120
HATING OUR CHILDREN   121
THE STARVED MAN   122
THE STARVED MAN GOES TO AMERICA   123
POETRY RULES OK   124
PEOPLE WHO LOVE US   125
JESUS AND THE PLUS SIGN   126
PSALM I   127
THE NON-VIOLENT BOXER   128
INTERVIEW WITH THE NON-VIOLENT BOXER   129

# BOOK 6
# LOVE AS THOUGH

THE KISS I JUST MISSED   133
SINCE YOU LEFT   134
PROPOSAL   136
MORE!   137
POEM FOR A FISHERWOMAN, 1983   138
TALES OF A DOMESTIC HEART   139
DOT AND DASH   141
DIFFICULT HEAVEN   142
SOMETIMES THERE IS A WAY   143
LOVE AS THOUGH   144

# BOOK 1
# VENTRILOQUISM FOR DUMMIES

## HOW TO SWALLOW A PIG

Because of the shape of its face, a pig is actually one of the easiest animals to swallow whole.* Still, pig-swallowing is a very difficult and potentially dangerous activity. If you have advance notice, a certain amount of jaw-stretching and lip-widening prior to the event is always helpful. Your greatest enemy is self-doubt. You have to look at the pig's head and tell yourself that you *can* do this. Once you have greased the pig, begin by letting the fine, tapered end of the snout proceed through your lips. The first obstacle, if it is not the back of your throat, will likely be your front teeth. Unfortunately these will have to be broken off. This clears the way for the full face-taper of the pig snout to zero in on your gullet. You have to be thinking "Outrage" when this begins to happen for it is entirely violating and painful. But your throat can take it. Allow the gorge to widen as though it were a fluid, thinner with each stretch. Your throat is a powerful python, infinitely elastic and accommodating. Once the entire pig head has squeezed by your gag reflex and entered your gorge, you are fully committed. You will not be able to vomit the pig out safely. Nor can you wait long to continue, for at this time your trachea is entirely blocked by the pig's head. You are unable to breathe. Do not panic. Do not attempt to gasp or retch. Concentrate on swallowing. Having the wideness of the pig's bulky shoulders in your once-narrow throat is perhaps the most violating thing you will ever experience. But you *can* do this. Just tell yourself, "This *is* possible." Swallow and stretch. Keep your lower jaw loose to prevent the bone from snapping at the hinge. Suck with your guts. Use your lower diaphragm to draw the fat pig ever further down the gullet. Let your thick and lucent saliva lubricate the way. Saturating the pig with your juices will allow the ciliated gorge to usher the pig deeper and deeper into your being. You may now need a friend with a stick to stuff in the pig's back end. This is the most crucial period. You will have been without oxygen for quite some time. You are probably blue in the face, but if you can widen to your most extreme limit, your throat cracking like wet bark, you will be able to slide your blue lips over the bare buttocks, and with the last kick of the back trotters, the curl of the pig's tail will be gone. The entire pig is in your throat. Your intestines are stretching. Peristalsis has begun. The glottis is finally released and the first, terrible new breath can come with a gasp. You've lived! You've swallowed the whole pig. And now that it's entirely in your stomach, ask yourself: "Is this not a most familiar feeling? Is this not the greatest feeling on earth?"

---

*It is also one of the easiest animals to shove up the anus. This is not recommended for reasons of hygiene.

# INSTRUCTIONS FOR LAUGHTER

It is not proper to go "Ha! Ha!", open-mouthed, squinty-eyed, pointing. Laughing can be executed with perfect grace, elegance, and still be 100 per cent expressive. Laugh with a straight spine. Let the kundalini energy come straight up and have its own little dance in the beauty of your face. Don't use laughing to shiver out disgust at your world, yourself, whatever lies are coiling too tight that night. Don't use laughter to sneak out some grief. Don't make hollow "Aaaw-aaaaaw" or "Eeee-aeee" sounds just to rattle some subterranean bit of the unused muscle of love. Don't stuff your laugh with terror bits. Don't push up a ragged laugh at outrage, or half-turn a laugh that ends in shock or shame. Don't laugh in a high voice like a puppy when you don't mean it. A laugh is not a bag you carry out the psychic trash in. You must not laden it with death-dread and toxic, boxy bits of brokenness. Let your body be a tickled trumpet-tit to the laughter. Let the giddy laughter play you like a tongue in the heart till you're undone. Laugh till your genitalia are laughing too. Let each vein mouth laugh. But do not brazenly bend over with your hands on your knees and scream. Real laughter can occur at volumes well below 12 to 14 decibels. It is uncommon for evolved laughter to continue into weeping, but this on occasion can and will occur. In such instances it is proper to wipe tears with only one hand — the funny hand. (Decide which hand is funniest and let it do the wiping.) It is considered vulgar to seek out laughter. It must come in the accidental course of living. Only this is true laughter. And so it is not proper to attend so-called comedy clubs, church services, or any reading, anywhere, of sacred vows.

# COLOURS OF BULLSHIT

Out of the brain pan, then, let us spread wide the colours of bullshit like a fan, and examine them one by one. First there is red bullshit. Red is the colour of the ardent bullshit of love that is always speaking. This is the kind of bullshit that gods listen to when they need a good laugh. As a matter of fact, gods get together in groups and laugh until they are rolling when they hear the words of people in love. If they hear an exclamation such as "O my love, my love!" it will cause them to howl. If this is followed by phrases such as "I won't ever leave you" and then a "Never?" followed by a "Never!", the gods will all shriek the word "Never!" together, almost hurting their throats with the intensity of their mirth. Then there is blue bullshit which is the viable bullshit of the day. This is the bullshit of scientists, statisticians, and psychiatrists. This kind of bullshit carries its own little tag but is nevertheless hard for the unpractised eye to detect. Listen for phrases such as "experts agree" or "statistics prove." Next in the total rainbow of bullshit comes green bullshit which is unhealthy and has lots to do with the bragging of young men in change rooms, business banter, and the sickly words of deliberate seducers. Green is the colour of advertising bullshit. It is the underlying tinge of World War II bullshit. It is the green of the goiter, the fungus, and the gangrene infection and is bottomed out only by that most despicable of all bullshit — white bullshit, which is of course the colour of recorded history. White bullshit is actually a very highly priced lubricant. The very one that keeps all those young bodies sliding into uniforms and all the pistons and gears of arms factories in motion. You have to be very careful with this kind of bullshit for it is a highly toxic, slippery, and explosive substance.* When you see it, recognize it. Call it by its name which is its shame. Say "Bullshit! Bullshit!"

---

*If you want to examine the colours of bullshit more closely yourself, you can safely do this by staring at the coloured pieces of cloth which are used to attach medals to generals' chests or simply by staring intensely at the flag of almost any country.

# PEACHES

Who remembers eating his or her first peach? Nobody! Why? Because peaches are for amnesiacs. In fact, the peach is a huge hallucinogen — a round tab of sunlight that induces visions of Utopia. To eat of it is to dream that humankind can, by well-directed will and intellect, move closer and closer to a state of "divinity." Repeated eating of peaches has led to some of the most benign leadership in all of history. Gandhi ate peaches. Mother Teresa ate peaches. Lennon ate peaches. When a bad peach is eaten, however, it is the whitest, weirdest side of the sunlight that slips into the mind's long hallways and meadows, and there the dream of love — just as you reach for it — triggers some destruction. There, if you sing of love, towers fall and murders occur. In such a state the only way to preserve love is to be immobile and ignorant. But to eat of pure peaches — pure, radiant peaches — is a delight unequalled in all the known satisfactions of humankind and is easily worth the risk of going mad. Indeed, it is said that some, when finally tasting their first peach, have swooned and writhed in the ecstasy of mere taste. Poets fed peaches are fat with packed-in light. They glow from a centre in themselves that is totally luminous and willful. They eat a peach and they write another poem. They eat a peach and they glow in the dark. Poets eat peaches and forget. That is why they write poem after poem. That is why there is always juice on their chins.

# MANGOES

In mangoes reside all the prime first kisses of passionate adolescence. These mango kisses are the purest, most uncontrived, unknowing kisses — kisses of forbidden love, red sunset kisses at dawn, hot kisses that bring down a pure glow of evening into the astonished mind. Mangoes preserve in a fine juice all that was best in everyone's finest romantic moments, and they leave the taster forever changed. If a man who has never tasted a mango tastes and shares one for the first time with a woman, that woman shall forever have for his longing all that is best of the world's kisses, and in seeking her love he will seek after the love of all the world's women. Likewise, if a woman shares her first mango with a man, she will see in his eyes all that was ever in the eyes of men and more. She will feel in his loins all the loins, all the lives, and all the loves that could ever be. Such a couple can never be parted and their happiness can only increase the happiness of all lovers everywhere. Nor is the mango itself reduced in this happy exchange, for in return for the wonder it has brought them, such a couple always willingly donates their best kiss to the mango's ever-increasing hoard.

# SWEET AND SOUR ANGEL WINGS

First you must set up a reading lamp and leave open a book of good poetry. You need the best poetry so that when an angel is flying by it will sense something and nip in secretly to read this curious dust — language. That is when, if you have put a trick ending on the poem, you can catch the foot of its spirit and slowly, with a blue buzz saw, cut off its wings. After you have removed the angel's wings you can let it go. No need to kill it, for it is now just like a man or a woman and even though it is suffering agony and hating you for what you have done, it will prefer the long suffering of life again rather than another immediate death.

If you are truly kind, there is a powerful ointment very helpful for the pain of wing-stumps!

Now pick the feathers from the wings and when they are stripped, cut them into book-sized chunks. The wings at this point are very delicate and should not be handled too roughly, for the marks will show up later as bright blue welts on the steaks. You will notice that there are many streaks of colour in the delicate flesh of angel wings. If you can succeed in cutting your steaks along the lines of pigment change, then you can serve what is known as "The Rainbow Banquet."

When the steaks are cut, roll them, while they are still puffy, in bread crumbs, then cook for 30 seconds in boiling honey.

One angel serves a banquet of 20.

# SECRETS OF PAPER

At night when you're weary and you want to forget, simply stick your head up through a piece of paper. Sleep in a sheet of paper and pull it up over you so that you cease to exist. Paper can be opened up like shale and a thin layer of pain can slide in dark and deep like a sliver. If your body is full of pain, if your heart is full of anguish, simply wrap yourself in clean paper and pray. Paper is a blotter to such things. Paper absorbs psychoses and silent screams. It is an endless realm and each sheet is a portable window into further eternities — white unwritten eternities, waiting for limbs, hats, heads to pop up. Look, there is a body in the milk! A great whale arising, an ancient civilization. Look deep into the milky lens of paper and realize why you can't just lie down and die. Because there is a trick alphabet at the bottom of paper that explodes — a deep electricity, thin filaments of feeling running out of sight to a white pool you can dive into from the heights. A forbidden milk. A detonator.

# PAPER

I have found a mad way of throwing bits of paper in the air — old newspapers, notes, and ticket stubs — so that when they come down, the reeds in them blow hideous melodies, unbearable vows, and long, lyrical strands of divine information. Paper is a whole orchestra, a symphony of milk. Just hold a piece up to the wind and listen. Shrill poems blow off its first layer like dust. There are synthesizer notes stuck in it like gulls. Now take a single golden hair, draw it across paper and listen to the depths of resonance you uncover in it — snowy canyons of bassoon talk, thunderous up-swellings of awe and wonder. We unfasten paper from its place in the wind and let it fall, hearing quite shrill, like a thin layer of pain, oil burning off in the cries of multitudes, piccolo shrieks of jet planes harmonizing on high.

Let us fill up the white balloons of paper. Let us all slash the paper like mad swords in the air and listen. We don't play enough with the music in paper. Our children struggle with tight pianos. They jinx their fingers on violins. Let them play trumpets made of paper. Aaaaah, while others toil at unwieldy instruments, let there always be this mad running about the house with a piece of paper on the end of a string.

# THE SCHOOL BEHIND THE SCHOOL

Certain people feel that there is much to be gained in life from an ability to sit together in neat little rows of about ten — five rows side by side. To this end, they have built large walled buildings and therein train their children from an early age to resist all the temptations there are to rise up and go outside and play. Initially there is an adjustment period during which they do not unduly aggravate the young ones, but very soon they begin to test the children's willpower with shrill chalk screams, cackling old ladies, and nasty men in square hats. If they can sit in these neat rows and learn to memorize facts for a period averaging 17 years, then upon passing a certain prescribed examination they are deemed to be graduates of the school itself and thereafter fit to be playground instructors, ministers of recreation, or revolutionaries. The entire education is not complete, however, unless they have passed the awful truth test. At some point during their endurance of the long training process, somewhere among history lessons, seminars on mathematics, and spelling bees, somewhere in the midst of all this the awful truth becomes visible to them for one searing second. If the child can maintain his or her composure when this happens and not rush from the room holding his or her head with both hands and screaming, the child will have passed the most important test there is, and shall then be considered a graduate of the school behind the school.

# SUBSTITUTE TAG: AN IDEA FOR A CHILDREN'S

To be played upon a fairly large field of green grass. The ⟨ is "it," whenever he or she catches and touches another ⟨ ⟩, shouts substitutions such as "rocks for honey and sing of bees."* The person so designated then, while effusing extempore** on doctored bee rhythms, shall attempt to touch and force a further substitution on someone else, such as "honey for alabaster and sing of ancient Egypt"*** or "alabaster for poverty and sing of her neck her neck."**** At the end of the game, when the last person has been touched, all the children, having stopped their initial composing with the touching of someone, shall begin again their effusions singing together faster and faster till they meet in the middle of the field, join hands, raise them up together, steeple-like and shout, "Hail, hail the dictionary."

---

* e.g. "The bees do make the rock the rock. They gather up the pollen to the hive and they do make the sweet rock, the sticky rock the rock the rock the rock."

**A Latin term meaning to compose spontaneously.

*** e.g. "Egypt with your honeyed urns, your flesh like ancient honey, sagging from your wicked old frescoes."

****e.g. "Aaaaah, your long lean neck as white as poverty. Yes, yes I want to pour your beauty into frescoes of poverty. To make from poverty a white model for the ages to come. To say yes poverty is beautiful, but have you seen her flesh . . ."

Plus: "Bleeders for leaders." "Salute, salute our great bleeders who have bled us to this mighty pass for we have been bled to the very gates of heaven, to the welcome door of hell, and there is no stopping. Even here, they will continue to bleed us. All along through the dire valleys of death they will bleed us unstintingly waving the red flag high. They will bleed us to the mountaintops and deep into the stinging salt seas. High and outward through the darkening skies we will be bled, hardly pausing to look back to see the long way we have come before we turn and face the clear pathways of tomorrow."

# EGGSHELL CHILDREN

Eggshell children are our most fragile and precious resource. They can grow into great diviners, discoverers of fabulous new lyrical machines. If they can grow into human reeds there will be a white kind of moonlit magic again. But with even the most tolerant of parents, an eggshell child is in constant danger. You see, eggshell children want to last forever. They want to be free and always have their own way. They scream and cry at amazing volumes and cannot be dissuaded from expressing rage, terror, and despair, and though they also excel at having fun, at bringing delight, there are times when their parents feel like handling them roughly. Usually much violence has been done to the parents in their own childhoods — but they are big, meaty, solid people, not delicate instruments of music like the eggshell child. One fist could cave an eggshell child in completely and it would lie dying, broken into fine blue shards.

This has led to a proliferation of forums on the care of eggshell children.

Here are some of the basic rules:

When they are born do not hold them upside down by the feet and smack their bottoms as this will ruin their little eggshell arses. Do not deliberately put them in rocking cradles on window sills in the breeze. Watch your subconscious urges with them; don't suddenly forget and clap them on the back. Don't throw them a rock, a hard ball, a spoon. Don't grab their hands when they try to run away from you. Don't pull their teeth out with strings and doorknobs. And, finally, do not slap eggshell children's faces in anger — this can not only completely ruin their cheeks, but also crush leagues and leagues of delicate diamonds in their eyes.

# HOW TO VISIT ME ON MY CLIFF TOP

I have placed several obstacles on the stairs. They are there to weed out the poor climbers. I wouldn't want anybody unsteadfast to knock on my door. So ignore the twenty dollar bill you will see on the bottom. Bending over will cause you to somersault ceaselessly in the air. It will always be exactly three feet from your hand. And afterwards don't whisper anything in the little ear. I put it there to listen to people's secrets — to report any unheard flatteries someone might have mumbled. But it hears only desperation, anguishes. Even the most heroic people have said "I hurt" to it. I guess it is one of my failures — a magnet for all your insecurities. On the next step I have left a completely random decoding device. Most people are stopped here. They can't resist putting their money into it. "What does it mean? What does it mean?" they ask. In return, obscenities are hurled at them — recipes from chili cans, old detergents, and chromosomes unaltered. (So I lost my best friend the Fuller brush salesman.) In the middle of the stair there is a totem pole with a star on top. Don't slash it. Everybody slashes. Especially the ones who got their crew cuts examined in the concentric circle unraveller. What happens if you slash it, is that quicksilver drips from it, and suddenly the weather changes. If you arrive in a flurry you will go home in a hurricane. Or a limousine. It makes no difference to the totem pole. It was carved from the blood of many dead pigs. The star is a very vain star. Attracted by the small uselessness of telescopes and then tied down. Most who pass by this step don't make it to the mirror. Don't stare in the mirror, whatever you do. For the mirror is also a telescope. All those shames — all those tiny zits and blemishes you thought were so far away from you — there they are, big as asteroids, fat, buck-toothed moons of you discharging and discharging. It is possible that having heard this you will tie your hands behind your back and look at it anyway just in passing, but the thing is, then you won't be able to carry the pyramid. And I insist that you bring a pyramid because then if there's a rather annoyed-looking blonde with me when you arrive you could just say, "O, I can't stay long, I just dropped in to drop off the pyramid," and throw it over the cliff and leave.

## TEXTUAL DIFFICULTIES

I will teach you that it's not enough to be infatuated with the word. You are in a textual relationship with language. It's not just about you. You have to be sensitive to the needs of the word — then maybe it will receive you. Otherwise you are doomed to its hardened exterior. The word will not open, the word will not enter you. This is the most common form of textual difficulty. Perhaps you are rushing the language. You may have to take your time with the poem. Or maybe you're taking too much time. You have to be like radar to the moods, textures, and shifts of the lingo. And don't get possessive. When you're "with" the word, you're with every word that word has ever been with. Accept it. All words are contextual free spirits. Practise on the smaller forms at first — haiku, aphorisms. It will seem impossible that one day something the size of *The Iliad* could enter you, but if you are patient — if you hold the words in your mind — if you let the word touch you — energy will enter. But you must also enter the energy. Hold the word as the word holds you. You must be taken. If you just take what you want from the poem then you leave unresolved charges simmering in it. This is how textual difficulties start. It is necessary to attend to the urges of the poem and to do this you must be patient and unctuous. You must focus and receive and let go entirely into the movement and rhythms of the poem. The key is mutuality. To get to where nothing comes between you and the language. To ride naked text, tissue to tissue. Wedged into a book like there is no exit. Full textual engagement will often, and some say should always, lead to those epiphany moments when insight like white light shoots up the being with a burst of raw alphabation. But remember, as important as it is that the poem satisfy you, this will only happen when you satisfy the poem. Only then will it fill you with the glories of literature. Only then will you be on your way again to a full and happy text life.

Of course not all your textual forays need be bound by such sweaty and arduous parameters. The lure of easy and casual text is everywhere. We've all experienced text in phone booths and washroom stalls, text up against the wall, or on public transit. You can't get away from text and you don't want to. Some people claim too much text can make you go blind, but the truth is text is legal and safe. In fact people have sacrificed their lives and freedoms for your right to experience almost any kind of text when and where you like. In general though it is good to give your words a periodic check-up. Let us compare dictionaries on a regular basis. Let us verify the language. Purify the word. Remember to exchange armadas. To do time in one another's subs. Whether you absorb the word or the word absorbs you, every time you speak a camel treads the needle eye. This is the true traverse of the double-humped dialectic. This is true textual intercourse. I give you my word.

## HOW TO CATCH A DEITY

Out of your eyes and hands make a hook, and of your words make a fine thread, and from your worry and secret heart make a reel. For bait, a book will do, a bit of cheese and salad. Now put out a bowl of glycerin and hang the smallest possible star over it. Perhaps the tiniest amount of cat-purr and elbow grease applied with a synthesizer. Now, before doing the God-call you must invest in a wisecrack for it to catch its tales in. When, at last, it comes to eat the salad, slip in your hook.

# THE CUP OF WORDS

It is interesting to watch the cup of words go from mouth to mouth. When the cup is first filled it is usually the politicians who go for the first sip of the cream on top. Thereby they get the words most prone to illusion. The words most fragile, most filled up with air. Then, when their mouths are full of froth, they pass the cup on and make great speeches. These usually come out at state-funded dinner parties when the cameras are rolling. It is the businessman who next dips in. He gets all the light-weight words — the graph words and math words that float to the top. If there is any scum he gets that too — a pure thin film of high class expletive condensed. Something to ream out at the secretary in private at the office or to mumble into tape-recorded messages when no one is listening. Then he passes the cup down to his comical sidekick the adman. The adman is pleased to get in at the very brimming-over of common usage. Pleased to dip his long tongue down almost to the bottom of the glass and savour every well-used syllable, each one resonant to him of sex. The cup is almost empty when the thirsty people get it. By then it is just the dross of language — enough for them to identify their grey clothes with. On and off buttons. Enough to say "fuckin' this" and "fuckin' that." Right at the bottom of the cup is the word "Revolt!" You have to be very thirsty to drink it in — it is a hard one to swallow. When the cup is passed back to the poet, he first looks at the bottom to see if that word's gone. If it isn't, he refills the cup and passes it on to the nearest Premier. Then he takes out a bottle of his own private stock, finds himself a flower or some butterflies, and proceeds to get very drunk.

# INK

In the beginning there is a huge canister of ink — ink that will find its way, by industry, to great fields of pens and be injected into them so that they are tall and ready and full. This is the ink before it is drawn out in delicate strands, in fine loops, in blots and stains. This is the ink cleaving unto the inkiness of itself, imperturbably blue, deep, and resonant. What desperations it will represent, every undulation of its being woven into finely worded anguishes, crude notes, and desperate letters. It will be neat rows of mathematics or strung out like paper dolls in signature — a thousand times the same name till one more column has run from its reed like water. Ink is almost like human promise in its untainted depths — it is a haze of possibility, a genetic ocean that all the rivers in letters run to and from — the blue loops of nonsense, the exact demands of separated husbands. Ink will stain the poet's chequebook and the eager ledgers of business with its azure abandon, running into preset forms, filling them with meaning and loss. I envy ink the transformations it will undergo — all the things it may be or represent — yet I wonder sometimes if all its curlicue adventures are terrors to it — long circuitous days that will waste it away with drudgery, leaching its life into meaningless syllables and useless words. Perhaps in such a state ink remembers and longs for its origins in the canisters of industry just as we, separate and adventurous, remember sometimes our unity in light, before we were bodies, souls, and egos. The days when we were all of a piece, caught up in each other like mutual bodies — the days when we were dark and thick and full and didn't mean a thing.

# BOOK 2
# FROM THE INTERSTELLAR LIBRARY ON ARCTURUS

# THE EARLY EDUCATION OF THE NUM-NUMS

Their word for love is impossible to pronounce. It has every letter in our alphabet in it at least twice. Their first and greatest art is to learn how to say it. And even then it requires a truthfulness and vulnerability beyond the scope of mere art. It becomes a way of being — at first just a ritual scrawl, then a riot of passions, a jangling of every ancient syllable in the loins. Even the crude phonemes of rocks and amoebas. Timelessly then, as they grow, it all comes together, this sound from this thing, this sound from that. Fatal wisdoms are acquired and then imparted, slightly lessened, with the drinking of them at them. Finally they acquire immunities. They need no clothes then. No appetites or lies. They show only the ugliest things they have in order to be cleansed of every vanity. Then, when they are entirely beautiful, they mutter that first important word, the first twenty-three letters of which translate as "I think I am ready." After that it is all a senseless cry, a reverberation of wild lyrical sounds into the night. Then the other one will appear. Just like that — the other one on the planet who has also just grown into the tongue. He or she will be there and they will wrap tentacles about one another, ready now for mathematics.

## FALLING IN HATE

In Xenophs, true romantics fall in hate with one another — often "at first sight." Peaceful, sober citizens will usually try to resist the overpowering tug of such mutual hatred but they yearn to be at each other's throats. They want to kick each other's heads in. Their loathing is long, unreasonable, and obsessive. They can't stop thinking of clawing each other's eyes out, stomping on each other's intestines. Hate letters bring no relief. Vile poisonous poetry exudes but never drains the green heart, the gritted tooth. Strong mutual hate can at first mildly distract but, ultimately, it debilitates. Interest fades in anything but the activities of malice. No matter how hard they try to deny their hate they can't keep away from one another. They are black mutually drawn compasses. They fall to each other like dark angels, astronauts of stone. Eventually, when they can no longer resist one another, they petition for an arrangement. They make mutual covenants before the law. Only then are they allowed unchaperoned into a dark room. There they finally have a go at one another. Until death do them part.

# THE ARMS RACE OF OBBAGGA

In Obbagga they have an arms race of a quite different kind. Obbaggans spend most of the year exercising their arms and fingers on treadmills and in galloping gloves so that on December the 19th, at the ringing of a bell, these arms can be chopped off and allowed in the shudder of their death throes, to gallop insensibly as far as they can. This is the famous Arms Race of Obbagga and it is watched by increasing numbers all around that planet. You can easily recognize the contestants, though. As the old saying in Obbagga goes, "They're the ones who aren't clapping."

# BEAUTIFUL MONEY

In Xanthos they have a new kind of money. Far from becoming more and more begrimed with its passage through people's hands, it becomes more and more saturated in their magic. Whenever a man, woman, or child handles this new money, they urge the good will of personal enchantment into whatever coins they hold. And, in being passed hand-to-hand, it will eventually contain all the good will of rich and poor alike. There are no faces on the new money. It is too soft for such a stamp and can bear as emblem only the fingerprint of whomever last touched it. The more this new money is passed amongst the people, the more beautiful it becomes, so that after much industry and much gift-giving and charity, it will be unbearably beautiful. Whenever this occurs, those who possess it are unable to resist running into the streets and throwing it up into the sunlight, shouting, as it falls and sparkles, "Look, money! Beautiful money!"

# THE ZELGS

## 1

The Zelgs speak in a language that is a cry. To hear them converse is to listen to the wailings, gargles, and gasps of those undergoing terrible tortures of the soul and body. To go amongst them, even in their merrymaking, is like walking the corridors of an actual hell. They greet each other with shrill enraged lizard screams, shouting till they cough up blood. And in instances where most people would choose to whisper — moments, for instance, of privacy and intimacy, the Zelgs will holler at their loudest volume (about 10,000 decibels). For them to utter some small, sweet nothing like "I love you darling!" is to bellow like Prometheus on the rock. Although the Zelgs are fine and sensitive creatures, it is obviously very hard for Earthlings to communicate with them. Listening to the simplest and most superficial discourse is heart-rending and will incite the compassion of all but the most dead and cruel creatures. Nor can they understand our small chirping and gesturing, thinking instead, that we only truly communicate when we torture each other.

## 2 TRAIDS

The Zelgs suffer from an epidemic of the deadly sexually transmitted disease known as TRAIDS which, for reasons as yet unknown, seems to attack only the monogamous. Alas, it can only be prevented by frequent, uncommitted, casual sex with strangers. Unfortunate as this already is for those betrothed in holy matrimony, it is made even more painful by Bacchic groups who use it to bolster their "vision" of a vast promiscuity amongst all peoples perpetually. These folks take delight in disseminating slogans such as: "Bareback is better!", "Gay is the way!", "We're bending over frontward for immunity!", and "Have you had indiscriminate promiscuous sex today?" And then there's their ubiquitous mascot: Bruce the safety goose.

## 3 ON FAST-FUCKING

In their effort to maintain immunity, the Zelgs put their extreme vocal abilities to a very practical use. I am referring to that practice known as fast-fucking, wherein the object is to fuck a stranger as fast as possible. The engagees (chosen by lot), after spending a day doing something slow and tedious, will approach one another as quickly as possible across a vast distance — usually a supermarket parking lot. As the actual duration of the fast-fuck is measured from the time they physically arrive at one another, participants will attempt to execute some manner of foreplay by shouting dirty talk to one another as they run. "Oooh I'm gonna fuck you so faaaaast!" is a big favourite. Or "In and out and it's over, baby!" Obviously the louder the voice, the more time it provides for such endearments. To augment this, on clear days, couples will also make lewd gestures and suggestive poses as they dash, ripping their clothes off in the process. When they finally meet, there is the quickest possible poke and hump, at least one brief orgasm and then it's over. The couple vow passionately to part forever. A promise they begin to keep immediately by dashing away from one another, full tilt.

# PSANTHOSIANS

Distinguished Psanthosian poets are awarded the "shit in the face prize." The winners are chosen by juries and warm, freshly dropped poop on aluminum pie plates is shoved in their faces. Although the manner of delivery is usually a simple straight-arm without crust, certain special winners are sometimes given the once-around-the-world, whirling on toe tips, grand slammer that knocks them right over treatment. Dark poetic eyes, blinking through excrement, are a commonly seen magazine cover when the awards are announced in January.

# REPORT ON THE EARTH-AIR ADDICTS

It is said that Earth-Air is at once the sweetest and the most addictive scent there is. That is why Earth has been declared off-limits to all our Fair Captains. We have lost too many of them — one scent of it and they abandon everything for the mindless comforts below.

Those who are addicted to Earth-Air often stroll. To stroll is to travel aimlessly — for "pleasure" as they put it. It doesn't matter to the Earth-Air addict — just a change of scenery is enough. For yes, most of the time the Earth-Air addicts just sit around staring. Just staring and breathing and sighing, examining with intense and seemingly durable curiosity such "fabulous" items as sand, stone, grass, or wave.

To be an Earth-Air addict is to abandon the star-search. It is to willfully glut the senses — to bathe incessantly in emanations. Just to go on breathing is enough — just to go on strolling. What a waste of life it is to become just a bag, a bellows for this detestable Earth-Air. Yet whenever our Fair Captains are missing we always find them standing on mountain peaks, breathing in Earth-Air. The wind blows and they are insane. They never want to leave. They want to run down into the valleys and breathe. They want to breathe all the different scents of Earth-Air there are. The famed Captain Zenon, for instance, was finally found perched over something called a "Daffodil," his mind gone, his nostrils flared. Captain Arbox was located in Ambergris just rolling and rolling, raving about the "aroma," taking great gusts of it deep into his lungs and then expelling it with long "musical" sighs that were terrible to hear.

# THE ENVIRONMENTAL LEAP FORWARD

I. I wake up and something amazing has happened to the parks. Something extraordinary has happened to those small squares and rectangles of trees and grass causing them to pop their borders and spill out, wildly exploding with green leaves, spear tips of grass, and all sorts of uncontainable flowers, wild fauna, algae, and strange medicinal herbs. After the first immediate alarm in the populace, this miraculous event is too quickly assimilated into "public" consciousness by the glib news media. Compacted into a catch-phrase and left there, immaculate and explainable, it was a strange "twinge" in the environment. "An environmental leap." Nothing to worry about. Just as we evolve, other things evolve "suddenly" and this was nothing but one of those periods for trees, grass, dandelions — dandelions everywhere impossible to weed out, great tangles of yellow sun-seeking dandelion heads butting at bank buildings and knocking over stop signs. The question now is how to get it all back to normal. How to begin clearing away these immense forests which have covered the canyons and prairies of everywhere everywhere and reassert the primacy of roads, ploughed fields, subdivisions, industry.

II. We have amazing images of the twinge that rocked nature. We have on video the burst of buds, the javelin hurl of poplars up to the point of that one highest blade of green quivering in the blue wind. Yes, yes, and look at the blur of these lianas, gentians, and violets. They are like purple blasts of rocketry, each blossom a trail of power left by something that has departed. Wow. And here is the mango grove that toppled the space fields of Florida, tangling up astronauts and gardeners alike in sweet exacerbating blossoms. I suppose everyone everywhere will always remember just where they were the day the greenery went wild. The night when nature throbbed.

III. Despite several years of effort in the tangled amazons of the River Don, the Toronto government has been unsuccessful in reestablishing the former Riverdale Park. Despite a massive government work plan to log the fabulous area and plant sod, efforts have been foiled again and again by the regrowth and the undergrowth of the powerful new foliage. Recently, a bold new plan has been put forth by city council to "integrate the city into the already-existing environment."

# SADNESS OF SPACEMEN

Some of them are not sad enough to be spacemen and so look down upon the soil and plant things in it. Some are so far from sadness they aren't even on earth but somewhere back behind memory where the two swamps are. Well, I am here to tell you that you can drop tablets in the swamps and they will well up with words. Listen to the artificial robins. The gazelles you have created. Does that sound like bird talk? No! It is the Ten Commandments. Followed by the Forty-Nine Commandments. And if out of the swamps someday should vast migrations of people come, with endless bowls in their hands asking for please just a little more, don't be surprised into saying "Yes." For they are continually voracious and will make of you an endless factory of jingoisms and bum-wad ads. So, finally put down your hyperventilating wallet. It will not now have to swim underwater to get to you. Instead, the ending is a joke. And if you laugh you get some seeds, but if you weep you must go out and begin to look for a rocket.

# BOOK 3
# ADVENTURES OF MY HAND

# CANDLES

You too have pulled a swindle and thereby gained those illicit eyes — that criminal vision into yourself. You, with your eye at the keyhole, you will see every jewel in the body: the heart, the many senses (more than thought), the mountainous fevers rising up from roots in your feet, the fear flung from you like a robe, and then, every night, by mistake rolled in again (just the dog of you rolling there), the vision seen then and again — later in the dream — the double-eye, the eye cluster inside, many times refracted and examined down to the last splay of light in the centre — the sphere of colour — and you too have a brush, or feet to dance, or even a pattern of blood, broad-minded, finger-painted in the whited cell — void monograms of God cast in sulphur, the unruly unholy ghost wrestling every other polter-geist to a standstill. You too can stand up on top of a mountain in yourself and be no closer to God because he is always under you. You have never needed humility to speak to him. O you with your eyes on stilts, yes, I know you see the small tender points of stars up there, but look — your toes are at the edge. Your body is waiting open-mouthed to receive you. Dive, you tall fool, from your black candlestick and be inside yourself like lights out. Each of us on stalks of pure terror keeps something inside that loves to dance in the dark.

# THE RETROACTIVE ORPHAN

I lost my job blowing on the windmills. I was too useful — somewhere lights were going on. Unluckily, I keep showing up on everyone's doorstep in a basket. Perhaps with puppies. Or that is what I'm told, and they draw the bulrush from the front lawn and, waving it over me, expect great migrations, a plague of frogs and flies, but I say to them, "No, I am not that orphan Jesus Christ, I am the anonymous orphan your son. See: I have the same terrible eyes as you, the same round basket of thorns at my side. Give me that bellows, that marking kiss we all run from, that line zagged across your face to the end of things. Give me that air and that light. I am here to inherit your gout and zits. When you look away from me, is it not as though from a mirror? Remember the big nose? The circular brow with its abacus of sweat and you up there — spider in your kingdom drawing in the beads like a miser. 'Work! Work!' you say to the hungry as they toil past you on the eternal pointless pyramid. 'When will it come to an end,' you enquire, pointing to the stuffed sky, bloated with your bricks and ambition. 'I only wanted to be eternal,' I say. 'Free from the clutched pocket the terrible hands of all potential stranglers and set them out to work on all the cords of God's thick neck. Wherever it stands or holds things up. Free the labours of the blood from its ceaseless treadmill.' I am that all-canceling zero. The big nothing at the end of the gauge. I am the powerful entrance to the pyramid. The point it will never reach. I am that instantaneous orphan of water. Just add me to your family and see how childless you are."

# THE ANCESTRY

I made myself a smooth oil for my parents so they could move better together. Many times they would not have touched if I hadn't come between them. It's true only the ugliest, the birds most bloated on refuse, came and stared in at our windows, and the neighbours thought my mother's singing was one perpetual scream. They had not seen the pencil marks, the stab wounds in my brother's arms. It was I who was singing — crazy as a loon in the basement, each one of my hands a web that kept me struggling over the past. For there was everywhere suction then — in and out. One day I would be blood red and four years old, another day just a sliver of myself waiting to pierce someone — anyone. Just like my mother who was always hacking at herself with the scissors, turning up face down in the bathroom sink, every drop of water threatening to turn red with her blood in my hand. And every time I see my father's face that fell down from the quarry, half of it carried off by the world for temples and the other half so lean with that one mad eye staring out like a Greek statue, I cry. There was no shadow I could lie down in that wasn't his. A statue, a tree, a mountain — each one of them owed something of their darkness to his nature. I fell to brooding. I plotted escapes. Perhaps there was a stone I could run into and be cool and silent forever. Or perhaps I could take on immensities behind the moon and suddenly emerge far bigger than he. But how my stem-mouth shrieked when he walked by me. I became excessively obedient. I bent even when there was no wind. Then, by degrees again, because it is my nature — innocent, arrogant, supersensitive — at one point, if someone as far away as a mile struck a match, a small glow would appear over my mouth and not fade for days. For a time I was almost always unbearably bright. There were fires everywhere and my father didn't like it. He said our family had a long history of water. It had always been good enough for them to dance, to sing, and fill things. No son of his was gonna be a flame. Then he threw himself on me and there was a big hiss. Luckily, just then, my mother came running out. "No Ted!" she screamed, and for the first time I saw the tiny flickering at the base of her throat: the impossible flame blood couldn't lead out of her but it glowed there forever with my blood and hers. Even there, where I was — somewhere the other side of burning — it reached me and my father said, "Alright then, he's your son, he's not mine."

# MY HUGE VOICE

I was born with a huge voice and I lay there with a huge voice in a new world, my voice too big for me. When I screamed I shook birds from the roof. My father called me "Big Mouth" and went to sea. My father came back and beat my voice and my voice got harder and harder. My mother grew my huge voice in a pot. She put its feet in the cradle and gave it a story at bedtime. As the body grew, the voice grew, larger and larger, stronger and stronger. Soon I was dragging this huge voice through the public school system, sometimes hardly able to fit through doorways my voice was so huge and so stuck in my throat, and though I rarely sang, though I only whistled, though I talked at normal volume, my voice was huge and I knew it. Finally at the age of twenty I began to let my voice go. My voice that was gigantic. Which if I screamed could shake temples, topple towers, and blast leaves from entire trees. Slowly I let my voice unwind. I let it shake and shatter as it welled up, lying back, blasted open, almost broken by the voice blaring up out of me. It is hard to be a body for a voice like this — a huge voice that wants to be heard everywhere. Sometimes I try to keep quiet and end up shouting. Sometimes I try to go to sleep, all swollen up with this voice, and it is too late to sing, too dark to speak, so I must lie there till the morning utterly silent, my body, an elastic to the sun, a small halter the voice is breaking through, my mind just a trembling seed for the wonder of this voice.

nily was one of those which had a halter made of leather the entire family could get into and wear. This was teamwork, my mother, my father, my brother, my sister, and me all strapped in and dragging the house through the gravel pit. Of course my little sister wasn't much help as she was so small and my mother was always suddenly bleeding at the eyes so this made our progress harrowing, but at times my brother and father and I were excellent huskies, going on long past endurance up the aisles and alleyways of Emotion City, a silver sheen of feeling caked in on the unclean streets, stuff you could slide in and be covered, a lament sinking in. Intense loneliness sinking in as you have your hour on the porch watching the strings of other houses going by, wondering why you don't have any friends. At night my brother and I would sleep, we would wrestle and fart in our rooms while my mother and father went at it deep into the night, dragging till they fell asleep, winding up all the toy TVs, toasters, and even the clocks which would all too soon wake them up.

II. I wanted to break out of the family halter though. It was too stuck in my heart and I was treated like an animal — a work horse. I wept into the leather of the halter. I bit at the halter always swearing to be free, to run off at last without this house in the suburbs on my back and the school books and the cups on my back, just to cut it all loose, let it slide behind me. Aaaaah the dives, the glides, the whips, the whirls I would do once I was free, cut loose in downtown rooms, lying in. But you need allies. There are always other halters waiting in the streets — industrial corsets, old educational buildings, trick flowers that will trap you and have you howling, caught on treadmills in the wind. You need allies. You need friends with sharp tongues, a book, a thought, a look that can cut like sharp hot steel. Slash open the veins of these halters, let us break out like marine animals from nets. Beware of lunging desks which will exert tendrils and capture you, pulling you screaming down to safe jobs and a home in the country. There are strange halters creeping over the meadows, startling old nuns and annoying sad professors, people caught up in suction hats, held down by heavy cloaks and gloves which manipulate. You must be very careful of the vases and countertops which can capture you — wild carpets and paintings on the wall. Army sergeants and teachers may come. Governments and employment schemes. Watch out for the religious texts with halters attached. Do you want to drag all the large institutes of revenge behind you? Do you want the domiciles and dormitories of murder — of insanity — the large blue wheel of education and ignorance? Break out of the halters of philosophy and standard usage, busting them up like dove-bits in the tightened air. You have to take a deep breath, fill the chest, the guts right up, and shout like a trumpet that shatters itself with the first true blast, "Fuck you, you bastards!"

# IN STUPID SCHOOL

In stupid school they hated our guts and taught us the stupidest things they could think of. Geography had France located in Namibia and the Persian Gulf a subject of the Mississippi. It was good to learn false geography, they told us, so that later when we were traveling we would have the advantage of not knowing what country we were really in. This would make us much more employable. Falseness and confusion were my two great subjects — to make up the past each time anew. They spliced together old clips, dull montages, the worst in humour, failed jokes, commentaries for morons, and told us that this was history. I can't tell you the tirades of ridicule they put us through. The taunts and insinuations that were hurled at us in the name of basic grammar. "You are scum. You were scum. You will be scum." It was insulting. For a religious exercise each day we were forced to bow and salaam to our desks, the boards, the teacher's hems, all the while chanting absurd prayers such as "Please let us go on being excrement. Please let us continue to be useless shit." All to convince us that the world was stupid. That it was run by the stupid. That it was owned by the stupid and you would be best to make yourself as stupid as possible in order to be fully employable when you were older. The problem was our innate intelligence. Some of us couldn't believe the facts put out by such schools. We tried and tried but we failed in our education. We could not get certificates which assured us we were stupid and so now no one will hire us. What a fate! While our more stupid friends secure jobs in offices and factories, we must stand idly by, too smart to do anything but collect the dole, the dole, the dole.

# ON THE ASSEMBLY LINE

Rage made me nervous all morning. All morning I had watched the automatic daisies go by me on the assembly line. Raging and raging. I was so sick of sticking on the stamens. For a dollar fifty an hour. Every once in a while I would pick up one of the lilies and it would be one of the true lilies — the kind with human or lion's blood in it — and would just hold it trembling in my hand. Wanting terribly to crush it. Even sometimes curling my fists into claws, just holding it there, trembling and trembling. But, as I say, my fear had made me useless. I had centuries of obedience to overcome. What would the tall pink pig wear to its wedding if I crushed this lily? The thought nearly overcame me. Can you imagine a wedding pig without a lily and not cry? For a while I forgot about Marx. I forgot about Engels. I was in fact blinded by my tears. By the time I had finished weeping there was a veritable garden there all bunched up on the assembly line waiting for stamens. Unable to resist the intoxicating perfumes, I threw myself back into the task with all the avarice and determination of a mystic and by afternoon was all caught up.

# AT THE DOCTOR OF FLAWS

All day long I dragged my flaws down Darcy Street, straining as I walked like a horse with a plough. I was craters, just flaws and flaws. None of them — and there were pimples there, epidermal cysts, pock marks and sores — none of them had the tiniest little bit of a wheel under it so that it was thus all drag. Indeed, so big was my heap of flaws that when I got to the Doctor of Flaws I could not get them all through his doorway and had to leave them in an ugly mess like a traffic accident outside his window. He looked down through his window with a telescope examining them a long time before saying, finally, "I'm sorry, there's not really much I can do for you. I could cut them up and mix them around but that would only make it worse. I could give you glasses that make them seem smaller but that would stop you seeing pain in other lands. Besides, they cause gross ear chafe. That leaves hypnosis. You probably wouldn't like hypnosis. You would never love a single bird afterwards and you could say goodbye to your intestinal fortitude. I would advise you just to put a sack over them and continue dragging. They are bigger to you than they seem, anyway." "But my mouth is down there with my bad breath," I protested. "I would surely die with a sack over it. I need my bad breath to live." "Well, you'll just have to learn to cope with it then," he said heartlessly. Just then I noticed, tucked away in a darkened corner of the office, a little heap all covered over in sackcloth. "Well no wonder you are a Doctor of Flaws!" I yelled scornfully and, taking out my flashlight, shone it brazenly on the heap. "No!" he screamed, shrill like a frightened young maiden baring her biggest underground mole. "Please!" But there it was — his wallet and hemorrhoid. His Exxon card and the long strings like beads of sweat and pimples. "Dirty filthy little pretender with a microscope," I cursed him. I would have elaborated but just then I was aroused from my fury by the shouts of a crowd which had gathered about my bad opinion of myself in the street outside. It was obviously a meeting of The Society for the Prevention of Ailments, for they all had banners and placards and were shouting slogans such as "Stop ailments now!

Did you know most deaths are caused by ailments?" I was so embarrassed I ran downstairs immediately and, having a little book of my finest poems with me, began to scatter them desperately over the heap. But it was no good. The pock marks began to devour them, the bad breath wheezed through. You could see my desperate eyes down there, staring up like lost children. "Ban the boil! Down with cysts!" people were shouting as I strapped myself back into the halter and began to trot shamefacedly down the street.

# ADVENTURES OF MY HAND

So far away as my pocket, as close as your breast, my hand cannot get to the banquet on time. It is coming in from a far-off place, on a rocket, on a train. My hand the worker — a gigantic fist kept in a stall, pounding in fury. My hand in a suit pretending to be a man on some luxury liner crossing its legs. My hand is a great poet always writing. I remember it coming back from the factory crushed in a machine when I was sixteen — a fat mottled rainbow, huge as the hand of a God — a great fist in bed. I remember it slipping like silver into those rollers coming out crushed flat — a white web of bones till the blood held back rushed in to fill it, to rejoice in its return, shocked, running over the broken vein mouths, bleeding ever and ever inward — a huge gush down from the wrist that would blacken and rot. My hand screaming. My hand in bandages — those fat purple fingertips, that burnt palm, that swollen wrist — all of me threatening to bulge out into this multi-coloured bruise. My hand Joseph. My hand Jacob and Christ and Neruda. My hand the rebel, the fist, tied down by a million machines but still rising in the air, still smashing down on the earth, snapping the threads, grasping and clawing its way to freedom. My hand is hunted now. It wanders over the world in search of its own kind. It goes from door to door trying to be joined up to something, knowing it is just a small piece of the puzzle.

# MY THERAPEUTIC COCK

Sometimes I think I couldn't go on if I didn't have my cock to laugh at. If I didn't get to go home sometimes and whip it out and have a damn good laugh, I think I might just have to pack it in, give up the slave trade, and do some honest work. Fortunately I have an absolutely hysterical cock and am able, by laughter, to exorcise my guilty business demons and just be alone with myself. Me and the mirror and my lucky therapeutic cock. Sometimes, looking at it, seeing where the base goes in there by the pelvic bones I am absolutely howling. Remembering the words of a woman at work who once called it "a musty little tuber of my male ego, a big fish-stinking one-eyed monster," I will laugh until the tears are rolling down my cheeks. Once I stood up and spun it 'round like a propeller or a Roman candle and nearly burst with mirth. Sometimes I crawl around on my back and look at it up there whirling and just scream. Of course I worry about the neighbours. What if they called the police? What if I am dragged out of here shrieking and hooting and pointing at it like some kind of madman? Cock! You monstrous comic! You old hag! So what I do is spread pictures of starving people, tanks and landowners, countries and their flags, old lovers, battered children and parents around me and then if anyone comes to the door wondering what the hell all the screaming is about, I just show them these extremely hilarious pictures and they understand and begin to laugh with me.

# PRECAUTIONARY CHANDELIERS

For some, luck has the thickest thread and it hangs them over the world like little Christs for a while. The bullets go bouncing in the grand ricochet — the pin-ball of America all lit up in neon and you never know when that thread will fray in a wedding vow, snap in a brake cable, or simply come undone in some madman's mind. For some, fate's thread is just the line a big fish snaps — or just the wire a puppet dangles from, for yes, all are swung on ropes 'round and 'round in a huge tangle like intersecting yo-yos. For others, no matter how consistently they turn, seemingly in balance, slowly winding up the long thread of their days into marriages and coffins, no matter how consistently they spin 'round their deeds, there will always be a chance of fate's big careen knocking them off course, over-turning families, sending children scurrying out in huge automobiles, launching astonished girls in cradles over rooftops, ejecting wives and husbands from living rooms with dogs in the big doppelganger. And so is the science of prediction, puffed up in computery and fed by stealth, employed at any cost as telescope to the well-established neighbourhoods. I warn you though, no matter how many times you sit in that armchair, no matter how many times you pace that circle, inserting the protection like clock-work, establishing the blood in concentric circles on the moon, no matter with what consistency you pace out the dull legions of your one day, there is always that small chance, some small snapping of something somewhere will send a grotesque item hurtling through your picture window — a gigantic Greek talisman perhaps, a white alarming dog, or a yo-yo of bones snapped by some punky God. There will be a ricochet at light-speed shattering the glass to crystal and great fish of flame leaping up. That is when, if you have been careful, we may see you swinging above them, safe in your precautionary chandeliers.

# SILENCE IS COMING

Silence is coming. Silence is coming. Over the steppes of Africa, right now over wild seas, across the pampas of Argentina. If you are in Atlanta, if you are in Berlin, Toronto, Montreal, alas, a silence is coming. I don't know what it is. It may be a wind without substance — but it is full of the cries of dead birds, full of the cry of the natives and it is moving up through the prairies of America. It is sinking in everywhere — a silence of buffalo, a silence of bison and whale. One day soon the silence will move over us and we will not at first notice it — at home in the vastness of the silence, but then it will continue for an hour and each of us, as though in a dream, beyond the reach of sound or speech, will gesture in horror at the soundless reverberation of our axes, the silent working of our machinery. The jets will go by and there will be no shrill sound. The radio will glow but there will be no static and no cry from the crushed animals who will stare up from their pain at us, the stabbed man's cry lost in the silence, the raped woman's scream absorbed in the silence, and infants born into a soundless world — a world where the dog's bark goes unheeded, where the bugles blow without warning and where even the clocks lack for an hour their steady and unstoppable ticking.

## ALL THE SOUNDS A SCARED MAN HEARS

All the sounds a scared man hears — what are they in the dark but the footsteps of many gods across a kind of inner floor. Yes, the tympani tapped in the mighty anthem, the patter of rain on a dry roof. These are impossible pauses in the beating between hearts. He who listens gathers in a long skein of veins long ago woven into monstrous patterns for the agony of gods. That is when, at the centre, small bloods may jump out and demand critters. But it is no good. Fear with his huge sponginess persists and absorbs. Nothing will put him out of the body, for he is a wise tenant warning you of accidents. He bloats you out, distorts your face in a tormented whisper, reveals to all the world the sickliest whitest part of your soul. But that is how it is — Him on his high throne with the crown of tears and everywhere like the dancing steps of majestic horses — those sounds.

# JACK THE INSOMNIAC

I am Jack the Insomniac, a kind of Rip Van Winkle in reverse. Twenty years of insomnia is fine, but it is part of my gift that I do not accept the gift. I resist wakefulness. I can't help it, when everybody else goes to bed I get lonely. I want to go to bed too. In fact I am dying to sleep. I do all the rituals well the walking in circles, the salutation to the sun, tense, efficient, now a hot bath stirred sideways, the brisk shit, the harried read, and now to dread to bed. Yes, I get in the bed and I lie down and then I remember the sleeping tea! I get up, head to the kitchen, prepare the tea and return to bed. Maybe the TV will help. There are talk shows on. These are sedative. Where's my Vicks? My tryptophan? I lie down finally and turn and click and switch and stick my head up one side and watch awhile like that. Then I click again till I think I must surely be getting tired. I lie flat now, the pillow under my neck. I take a deep breath, forgetting who I am, and think I'll just listen and click, not that, click, not that, click . . .

It's been three nights. I can feel a big ball of sleep submerged in my being, luxuriant, enticing but impenetrable. Several times the ball wells up, overwhelming the little bit of mind, an image dancing, slides, I might just take this ticket but no, click, remember I am Jack the Insomniac. If I am not asleep by two I'll take the tryptophan. I can still sleep four hours, be up by six and my world is dancing, but I just missed that ticket. There is a small magnetic sound in the house and I remember. I need the fan on. I get up, creep in the other room where people are snoring, lovely faces opaque with desire, destiny, inner alertness, comfort and dreams, and without envy I remove the fan, take it down. Aaaaah. That will probably do it. I lie back down. If I'm not asleep by three I'll take the tryptophan. Aaaaah the luxury of sleep. To live in instantly created environments tangential to the worry, the hassle, the domain, the plentitude of the sleepless one. When will he accept that he is vibrating? When will he accept that his spine stands straight up above the bed like a divining rod to his soul shouting, "Son of water, you are Jack the Insomniac"? I have danced in a lyrical way the world would love and just as I would come down skidding, madly sliding into sleep, I slither, I scrape, I stop. There is a sound or a moment in the throat that draws me up again out of the fertile water, still hooked to the sharp curve of the night when I lost everything, gave up comfort, rhythm, vitality, to become a guardian, a watcher, a werewolf. My being vibrates between the two worlds. Some of it in, some of it out. Bits going backward, bits being erased, bits not even making it to memory or moment at all. But they're all there and fucking awake anyway. I begin to pray: please God help me, please God let me sleep. I want to go upstairs and apologize to my children. I want to wake up my beloved and weep of my love for her. I am a much deeper being here. The wave has had to come up into this world to get me. A giant on the thin bed, this man who fell out of time, opiate-eyed but wide awake. What a blossoming to strip off the skins of sleep seven layers deep to enter this new life naked, but what I'd give to spread wide at last these two leaden wings of insomnia and fall.

# PORTRAIT OF THE ARTIST

The "artist" enters stage right. Stage left, a large television monitor faces him. Beside it we see some recording equipment, a camera, and a small black box. A black bar stool stands centre stage in a tight spotlight. If the audience makes any noise when the "artist" enters, the "artist" shushes them severely. The "artist" should be prepared to be forceful in obtaining complete silence in the hall. When the crowd is quiet, the "artist" turns away from the audience and aims a remote to activate the audio recorder and the camera, stage left. We can see by the movement of its lights that it is now recording. Sitting upon the black stool the "artist" looks into the camera and tells the following joke:

*Question:* "What does Minnie Mouse say when the phone rings and someone asks, 'Is Minnie Mouse there?'"

*Answer (in a high mouse-like voice):* "Squeaking."

If anyone in the audience laughs, the "artist" turns toward them quickly with a very offended "Shush." Using the remote, the "artist" stops, rewinds the recorder, and retells the joke. Again, if anyone laughs or shuffles, the "artist," ashen with affront, begins anew. The "artist" retells and rerecords the joke with varying emphases until satisfied with its delivery. The "artist" then dons headphones and watches a replay of the performance. If it is still to the "artist's" satisfaction, the "artist" turns the monitor toward the audience and plays the recording of the joke for them. If the audience laughs or applauds, the "artist" is incensed, the nostrils wide-flared, quivering with rage. Only when the "artist" has played the recording to utter silence in the hall does the "artist" aim the remote toward the black box at the back of the theatre, unleashing deafening canned laughter.

When this is over the "artist" bows toward the audience, signaling that the "performance" part of the presentation is over. "Are there any questions?" the "artist" asks, smiling, at audience. If anybody asks a question the "artist" screams with frustration and stomps off the stage in a rage.

# BOOK 4
# UNSTABLE FABLES

# LIVES OF DAH

He cried out "Take away my pain" so they covered him in stars. Still Dah hurt and again he cried "Take away my pain" so they made time and put him in it with many clocks to wind his great pain onto, but the ticking only maddened him and he cried out "Take away my pain" so they made the big sack, memory, for him to stuff his past into, but it only increased the area of his pain so they took away his frontal lobes and with x's for eyes he said "Still I hurt" so they took off his flesh, but the pain was deep and he begged them "Take away my pain," so they tried to track down the pain but the pain was everywhere. "Take away my pain" he cried till finally they had to melt the white snow of his body. Yet the water ached, stricken of its individuality, each sparkle cut the eyes with agony and to taste of it was to drink dissatisfaction, eternal longing.

"My pain!" the water screamed. "Take away my pain." But it was too late; it was already evaporating. And the agony was piercing. It was already running off, saturating everything. "My pain!" the grass cried. "My Pain" echoed the river bed. "My Pain!" the rain raged and then the terrible thunder spoke Dah's name.

# THE UNFORTUNATE GENIUS AND HIS "WINKLE"

For your sake I will say that it was a "penis" he had and that it was fairly normal by most standards of height, breadth, and cleanliness. The problem was that his mind was abnormal — his eyesight was peculiar and his self-esteem small, such that whenever he perceived this "winkle" as he called it, it appeared minute, ineffectual, virtually useless, and embarrassing to him. No matter how much he put it up against the yardstick and measured six and a half inches, it would make him weep. "Why me?" he would whimper. "Why am I one of those who has to be born with a smaller than average winkle?" Of course he had read all those books, manuals, and magazines that said six and a half was average, but it was no good. He couldn't believe it — he knew who had commissioned and written those studies. Sometimes he would look down and it seemed just a little pink wick-like thing — something you would have to examine with tweezers. Perhaps this ailment of his was not peculiar. Perhaps all men have such doubts. But his mind was abnormal. He was, in a way, an explorer of the self — one of those who could, in desperation, run through strange visions into the endless riddle of his own creation. He could go under in the dark waters of self and come up from dreams in control. It was by this method, through willpower and determination, that he finally reached the source, the very centre of his regeneration, and there, through sheer brilliance, through unheard-of intellect, he reset the winkle control so that its stalled growth function would continue. He never doubted for a moment that the next day it would be infinitesimally bigger. And he was absolutely right. And so on the next day. And the next. After about six months of this he had a real big whopper on him. A great big pink wang of a winkle that he waved at himself merrily in the mirror like an ape who has finally figured out his first blunt stone. Soon he would be able to go out into the world of sex, he thought. Soon he would be entirely adequate, esteemed, even talked about, ogled over. And of course, as usual, he was right. Wearing tight pants he became desirable to a lot of women who liked the feeling of "being full right up" that a big winkle gave them during intercourse. For a while he was much happier. He realized though that sooner or later he must remake his velvet journey into inner peace and remove the stone of his command. After all, he didn't want his winkle to get so big it became unruly and unnatural. Alas, by the time he tried this, the way was blocked, the former passes all impassable. Everything had shifted and restructured itself. There was a huge happiness in himself now to support. How could he, drained by it, venture into that canyon of agony again. "So wait," he said. "Wait till you are unhappy. The way will be clearer then and the will stronger." So he waited and his winkle grew to the point of becoming a little unsightly. Now only the most bizarre of those who liked to feel "filled right up" came to him. Others began to regard him as something of a monster. He enjoyed their awe for a while but he knew the winkle was just getting bigger and bigger and more difficult to inflate for sex. Was he a little jaded? Sucked out by the excesses of his recent life? Time to exercise the inner muscle, he thought. But it was no good. The way inside was still blocked, almost as though some genius had built a wall against him. Still his winkle got bigger and bigger. He discovered for a while that if he diverted all his other energies against this energy he could slow the rate of growth. But this meant having his mind filled with sex and gender and coitus, and all its words and synonyms. During this time you couldn't talk to him without him suddenly saying, "Ah yes, I remember, I parted her lovely fucking cunt and poked my great big fucking winkle at her and she fucking grunted and I squeezed it in a little, like it was a snake going down a fucking elephant's throat and I fucking humped and she fucking heaved and . . ." On and on . . . At first some of the more machismo men would join in with him, but soon he was too nauseating, too single-minded even for them. Still the winkle got bigger and bigger and one day when it began to erect, the blood drained out of his head and he passed out only to wake up in hospital. Here he was lonelier than ever before. After a month the winkle was as huge as the rest of him — a great, flaccid, pink stinking thing that even callous hospital officials and nurses couldn't bear to look at, but had to keep always in its oxygen tent, pumping in the blood. Soon the rest of him began to wither. It was the law in that place that a person must live as long as anything can possibly make him, so they kept him on the heart and lung and kidney machines. Finally the rest of him just got eaten away by cancers and you could just barely see, hidden in the tumours, his crusty old face, withered there in mortal agony. When, at last, the eyes closed forever, they encased him in a huge box and ten men carried it to the immense hole they had had to dig to put it in. After they had said their prayers over him they put up a tombstone which read: "Here lie the remains of a great big Dick."

# THE VANISHING BRASSIERE

I. The vanishing brassiere hung down in the conscience of the "monogamist" with no tits to fill it. If he thought of "Fuck," it was the wind whistling over a razor's edge, "FFFFFFFFFF," and then a tympani of nuts falling onto tin cans, "K-K-K-K-K-K!" Like the cratered eyes of some dog he'd maimed, that brassiere haunted him. When would it reappear and relieve him of the ballast of his guilt? Always, no matter what he was doing, he was searching for it and everything that came between him and finding it easily was a razor. The clock was a razor. Every evening was a razor. His wife was a razor — especially his wife, whom he had used over and over again without, he thought, in the least dulling her wit. It was still pebble sharp. But how she slashed him from the mainstream. How she cut him at the wrist of the world. How, where fits should be stuffed in the brassiere, she left only blobs of conscience congealing with his cries. One day he would come home and it would be like a corpse in the closet. Stuffed with two denials. Perhaps one a little bigger than the other. Or he would suddenly see it in a corner of the bedroom like a distant goggle, eyeless at his passion. One thing for sure, somewhere it was waiting viciously to devour the small security he had. Till then, till that last supper it would make of him, daintily he danced on the razor.

II. After the judge had examined all the tiny marks of countless keys, the lock of lips left undone at her mouth, the red welt about her neck where she had been his boutonniere, he asked, "And is the other woman present in this courtroom?" "Yes she is," the wife replied, lifting up her finger to point. She had a truck tire for a wedding ring on that finger but still she pointed. She pointed at what appeared to be a huge piece of Swiss or Limburger cheese at the back of the courtroom. "No! No!" cried out the "monogamist," jangling a tiny foetal skeleton unconsciously in his pocket. "She is just a razor. A razor. A razor. And you, judge, you are a razor, and my hands — they are both razors and they both cut at me, and every woman to every man and every night in every bed is a razor, a razor, a razor, a razor . . ."

III. For alimony she got one nostril anvil. Two avuncular aunts without morals or tongues. Three black and white zoot suits with armless and legless dependents in them. A team of interlocking dog legs. A cheese player (stereo) and a yogurt recorder with matching cassettes. A mouse that wore knuckle-dusters made of fetlock and sheep dip. A ship with and without an asshole. Something quite humorous. A lobotomized tomato, a month's subscription to *Lock and Bar*. And last but not least, a manila envelope full of circles that were not round. These she put up on the wall, pretending sometimes in her agony and solitude that they were holes winds whipped through when, in the dark, she seemed to feel a chill.

# HIS LITTLE MOTHER

I knew a man who wore his little mother on a chain 'round his neck. You might say she had pierced ears. Often she would turn around in rage and bite him, but due to the fact that he had tied her little hands behind her back, her teeth couldn't harm him. As can be expected, this strange behaviour of his did not prevent him from adopting all the newest philosophies of the day. Indeed, this fellow even claimed to be what is called a "Women's Libber." So eloquent was he on this subject that he was regarded as something of a saint. Yet, even as he spoke, even as he decried aloud the centuries of cruelty and injustice to women, he would raise his hand to his chest as though in religious gesture and begin to pinch his little mother. He did this so that her tiny screaming might add fuel to his rhetoric. On those nights when he did not bring liberated women home to fuck, he would untie her long enough for her to call him an ungrateful bastard. "I'm sorry, mother," he would say serenely, "but whatever I am, you have made me. Now go and do your business." After she had done her business, he would clothes-peg her little legs together so he could get to sleep.

# LITTLE HURTS

Little hurts gather in his brow, waiting to go "puff," waiting to go "pop" in a face of rage. Little hurts burrowing down to make room. Compressed voices, things he should have said. Aaaaah, little hurts like grain inside, like fields of broken barley, like dots pushed out. Little hurts on the bead a string of sweat provides. Little hurts on the abacus his fingers move along in dream-time. He is a water that life has plunged to the bottom of, his hand a catacomb of pain, his body honey-combed with grief, with little hurts like pellets, like moles, like darker eyes within his eyes.

# TEXTUAL PLEASURE

For the first time, the man is alone in the room with the book. Upright, closed, it leans on its bottom edge into the special shelf, its orange spine facing out, its text tucked neatly inside the titillating cover. Knowing it is in the room, there is a pulse in the man's body that doubles instantly. He almost feels sick at the intensity of his heartbeat. He walks all around his apartment not looking at the book. The erection he had initially has softened somewhat and he is dribbling a bit down his thigh. He can sense that he might be able to have a good one.

He takes the book into his left palm, face up. He runs his fingers along the top outside edge of the book's hard cover. He exerts only the very slightest pressure inward and upward — more a question than an action. When he feels the cover give and lift slightly, the man is again hit with a heavy pulse of lust. He knows he is going to open the book. He slides his other index finger down the back of the spine till it curls under the tail end so that with a gentle motion he can the tilt the volume back and open into his waiting palm. Wanton, the book's front cover now leans wide, exposing a searing whiteness. There is great delicacy, almost tenderness, as he runs his finger up O so lightly around and around the surface of the blank front page. Imperceptibly the circles grow larger, moving closer to the edge. His breath is close. He is blowing softly upon the uplifting paper. He sees the flash of black curling text on its undersurface. He is completely hard. He wants to just yank the volume wide open — go for its middle pages, but for the book's sake, he draws it out. He follows all the protocols. He lingers here at the lip where the words are slow and compelling, calling him on. His tongue touches just the tip of the first syllable of the first word and a sound dissolves in air. The book grows visibly warmer. The pages, if anything, spread themselves wider apart, expecting a full and delicious reading, wanting to take him into their deepest recesses. All the while as he reads he gently rubs his middle finger over the base of the book's spine, sometimes curling 'round and up into the tight wedged interior. The faster his eyes rake off the electric syllables, the quicker he hears the pulsing inside. Is it the book or him? Blood is rushing through something. The book is visibly engorged, lips swollen, reddened, the text stretched in places. The book has begun to glisten. The dots bulge atop the i's, the o's almost exude invitation as he buries himself deeper. And now the book has begun to read him. Some sensory faculty enlivened by his observation peers out at what is written in him, what the strings of gut say when stroked over. The man is right in the steaming centre of the story. The text washes all around him. Boat and sea are one. Eyes and text are one. There is no point where the man and the book are separate. Two sexualities collide and consume and magnify and multiply till the text is oozing from the man's pores. The book has read him right through to the spine. He is crackling with code. He is coming undone in his centre. Still the book reads on as he reads on. They've got each other by the root. They're deep under the tale of language. They're utterly gripped by one another, can't put one another down. Friction, fiction, there is no difference. They rub away at one another, scraping off the thin last skin to the breaking light below. The book erupts. It bends back and groans, its spine cracking. The man groans. Suddenly there are words everywhere awash in language and not language. Silence and not silence.

# FABLE OF A FABLE

He is running and he has the fable. The only fable. Not knowing even that there could be other fables — only this fable about the father and the mother and the land and the stars and the many, many wolves. It should have no weight, no mass, no backend, but it weighs him down when he runs, launching small parachutes from the back of his mind. It slows him down but he needs to deliver it. If he told himself the fable he would have to kill himself. It must reach all the people at once. An equal-opportunity fable with due notice to all. He doesn't know there's a malfunction in the fable, and though it's tiny, this flaw will grow. It should have been streamlined and easy. It came so quickly but now it has begun to rend the universe a bit. It has sunk its teeth into the obvious and already a few things are askew. The potential is awful. Already the people are gathering. Soon there'll be no snow, no cold to prevent this. He's super sleek. He's fabulized. He's chrome. He's sharp. He shines and that's the way he was designed, so he runs while the fable rots in his head, poisoned, unstable, more and more unstable — full of a terrible physics which might leak out. And they are dropping the sky on him. They are rearing up the oceans against him, but there's really no stopping him, so they have to stop the people from listening. But before they can get the first word out, he arrives and gets the first word out and that's all it takes.

# BIRTH OF A TREE

Recently a woman gave birth to a tree. Imagine the amazement on the faces of the delivering doctor and nurses when the first of the blue branches began to peek out. Each time the mother moaned and screamed, more and more of the undeveloped twigs, stunted branches, and tiny little leaves came curling out. When with a great push the trunk had finally been passed and the wideness of the base emerged, the roots followed with very little effort and the delivery team stared, amazed and frightened at what had come into the world.

Immediately upon being delivered, the small purpling tree began to writhe, shuddering and shaking. The tiny roots and branches convulsed, clenching in and out like multiple fists, and then the tree let out a cry. A cold lizard-like scream of anguish which seemed as loud as the shriek of a jet plane. A deep jungle kind of screaming, an ancient anguished swamp-infected note that shook everyone with the resonance of its agony. The doctors and nurses stood helplessly while the tree screamed, louder and louder, the blue limbs bucking in the sheets, the leaves shuddering like hearts, like broken mirrors, quivering and shining in the bright hospital light.

They were frightened by the hideousness of the baby tree — almost incapacitated in their task, but they were professionals and somehow managed to care for the needs of the mother.

When it became apparent that, by some miracle, she had not suffered undue internal damage from the birth of the tree, but seemed neither more nor less torn up than from the birth of a normal child, she began to cry, "Please, please, help my baby, my baby." For the tiny bruised-looking tree was starting to split itself open with the exertion of its weeping, coming undone outwardly with a fleshier and fleshier appearance, howling in horror and agony. Thankfully, one of the attending nurses then had a great flash of insight. She wheeled the tree over to the mother so that she could reach out her hand and touch it for the first time. There was a clemency, a cold distilled feeling in the air, a sound — almost a hiss, and then abruptly reassured, the frightened baby tree became quiet.

# THE MISUSE OF CRADLES

The thing we call a cradle is actually a very ancient invention, a secret configuration designed by a holy scientist who died a second before she could explain its great use to her king. For years it sat where she had left it, powerful and mysterious — a device which could, it was said, if properly used, utterly change the world. In an attempt to unlock this secret, the king had cradles installed in every home and made a proclamation that anyone who could devise a method to make them work would be rewarded with great wealth. Thereafter you saw cradles put to every kind of use — cradles high atop the aerials, cradles flying through the air, cradles in waterwheels, on tree tops, cradles housing lions, bears, bombs, rockets — all to no avail. Eventually this ancient king died and, there being no use for them, all the cradles were put in attics. Then new kings came, and newer kings, and kings of a different name until everyone forgot the cradles and the king and his contest. It wasn't until much later that people rediscovered these ancient devices and realized that whatever else they did, they were very good for rocking babies in — a practice which has continued to the present day. And that is the true history of cradles and an explanation of the secret in the nursery which gives every mother (if she can only learn how to use it) immense and incredible power.

# THE LITTLE SINGER

The little singer was a miner in the flames, a sun-denizen. He was a silver thread weaver. Ten times a night he wrapped it around the world. Now, a spider in lullaby, he hangs from the aerials turning and observing, growing full in the moonlight, holding communion with comets and crows, singing that endless melody of his, a melody that haunts and stays with you — a melody of eternal sadness. The little singer is an angel transplanted, a victim of a new divine science, he is a harp in skin, a trumpet in bones. He is a reed with silver hair, a bold boy of ivory, singing high and sweet and horribly sad above the rooftops. We watch TV and we see this little singer, his image doubling over the game shows. The little singer is there for the sports, unbearably bright in the sun. The singer is there in the newscast. His song filters through the radio from any channel — the star child, the little singer. Nobody can get the melody out of their head. People find themselves singing along, and then curse themselves, reminded of a deep sadness. They can't bear it much longer so they go to cut him down. They go up with scissors, with garden shears, with knives and razor blades and quickly they cut the slender thread that keeps him turning up there in his chrysalis. They bring him down into their homes and put him in one of the cradles. Still he is singing. He sings all night in the cradle and the house is full of his song. Everybody sings his song in their sleep and wakes up sad. Everybody goes to the cradle in the morning and the child is silent. He is asleep, the stardust all over him beginning to fade. The child is becoming one of us. His lips still move in sleep, still singing that melody. You can almost read it on his lips. You will never forget it but he will never sing it the same again. He wakes up and looks at you — his mother, his brother, his father. You all come to kiss him. You welcome him into the family. You cleanse the last strands of web from around his eyes and begin teaching him how to speak.

## A VERY LEAKY FAUCET

One evening a rabbit shadow dripped from my faucet and was joined in the middle of the room by a lot of other shadows, forming a mass of darkness. But where were the creatures these shadows came from? A whole cow dripped from the faucet, the buffalos, the pigs lowing, God, there were eagle shadows in the room, zeroing in on the centre of that ever-glowing darkness. I felt the run of cold calf's blood, veal-like in my bones. Soon the cock will crow and the room will be full of darkness, a detached darkness that can't get lost, won't ever disappear, only light going into it and never meeting eyes. The eyes are gone wandering now, or, axe-weary, have fallen at last into dust. Lo, lo you cattle of the cutlery, you haunted sheep of the living room. Soon there will be no place to hide. All the darknesses will be filled; no Christ of the animals to drain you out through the loopholes of love. O animals, gather in the kraal of my ribs your once-rich voices and we shall speak in the language of herds. But then, I thought, what if people gather in the streets and walk together, sure of slaughter but following anyway? Not willing to go with this, I made my way over to the faucet and with all my might turned the tap till I heard a screech of closure. There was a tense moment of hesitation, outrage in the pipes, and then the dark migration stopped, leaving me with this mewling ball in the middle of the room. I waited until the sun set, until the darkness in the room was no different than the darkness of the gone animals. Then, walking through them, almost seeing them, darker than darkness, grazing on my carpet, I opened the window and, by turning on a fan, ushered them screaming into the front yard. Where, to my knowledge, they were at last completely absorbed into the general night.

# THE PIG WHO DISCOVERED HAPPINESS

The pig who discovered happiness didn't tell anyone, not even the other pigs. It just lived a life of perfect glee dancing in meadows like a lamb, scooting up trees to sing from branches out of sight — a completely happy pig. And not a stupid pig by any means. This pig knew what was coming, but even that didn't affect its delight. It could have been an historic pig if it liked — a Leif Eriksson of pigs, a Columbus of pigs, and yet it remained a pig that never once tried to reveal its happiness to other pigs. This would only have decreased its happiness. This would have involved it in endless arguments. Better to be quiet and happy, the pig thought. And so, if bad weather befell, if tragedy struck, still that pig could be gleeful. And even at the very end, as it was marched to the abattoir, with all the others squealing and shrieking with fear, even then this pig kept quiet the great secret of its happiness. Not until it realized that its time was coming — not until it knew its own happiness would at last be ended did it attempt to tell the others. As they strung it up by the foot to slit its throat, it began to shriek in its high pig voice, letting out, alas, too late, that long-held and, by then, unintelligible formula.

# THE LITTLE PIG OF SELF-RESPECT

The little pig of self-respect got away from General Li Tu. It ran greased and squealing through the populace as the soldiers tried to catch it, leaving the general with a pig-shaped space suddenly missing from his heart. Immediately the weasels of remorse began to burrow in, looking for that absence. Hedgehogs of guilt and bloodfish of anguish long held at bay sucked their way along his veins, up through the marrow, all looking for that small shivering pig-space, to live in its emptiness, to take up residence in its vacated temple — the general, left writhing, sweating on the bed, beset by terrible visions, knowing there was no more pig-space inside, just a crammed banquet hall full of ravenous mice, and gorged weasels toasting each other with his blood. No more pig-space in the soul! Afterward, when the little pig of self-respect was dragged back to him, crying and squealing, he had nowhere left inside himself to put it. He had to wear it, stitched down, over his shoulders, like a kind of pink epaulette.

# THE VIOLENT MAN'S HAND

The violent man's hand fell into the dust and withered to the size of a seed. Later, from that spot grew the wheat that would be ground down into the earth by armies, the grains that would be burned and turned back to earth in peace.

The violent man's hand fell into the heap and from it a bird burst — a bright bursting bird, a third bird, a herd of birds, so that the hand leapt and spattered as each bird burst from it. Finally it was a spent black splinter from which blue sparks leapt.

The violent man's hand sank into the earth at two miles per hour, heavy as lead. To come back as a bomber angel, dark Lucifer jets with arms full of crosses and gelignite, bleak bomber angels, that only to look into the eyes of a newborn child can bring down, one by one — dark flies, dark fear-flung fists overhead, the severed hands of those who would strike us, dark wings of surrender, bleak hands of poverty thrown high.

The hand that was nailed up, crossed down, crushed at the foot. The hand that went mad and took on rage like seven gravities. That is why there are holes in Arkansas, call them comets, call them what you will. There is rage in those hands when they come down and the children run inexplicably past certain houses, terrified of a sound no one else can hear.

# THE MAD HAND

Once there was a floating walking hand which went 'round and 'round the world darting and crawling, hoping to evade detection, sometimes scaring drunks and small children. A wild leaping scampering hand not wishing to be part of a circus but utterly mad, knowing only old routines and concentric habits like circles at the bone — to dance, to tap, and insanely, to shake hands. That's why this hand took to creeping into embassies and literary parties, so that it could crawl up table legs, wait for the right moment and then dive into a handshake, usurping the place of the intended other hand with a shrill kind of scream. This is the hand that madly signed papers over and over again, pouring wine glasses back into nothingness, tilting back beers, making its stump shriek like a whistle.

For a while the hand hung out with spiders thinking it might be one of them. It dreamed of running over buttons like a minefield, setting off sequences of roses in some drunkard's head, detonating poems like Q-blasts. "Arrrrgh! Take me to the abodes of people! Get me into a glove! I will buck and jolt. I will seize up and spit blood if I do not get involved in a caress."

One thing the hand liked to do was grope and poke at parties — touch people in places no living human being could get at — give a poke in the dark and then roll across the floor like a combat-trained creature, chuckling with sheer unbearable squeals as the puzzled party-goer nervously eyed whoever was behind him.

Sometimes the hand liked nothing better than to ride the still surface of a stream like a water spider — to just hang there above its own reflection, each finger, as it touched the mirror, leaving a poem to the sky, an ode to the sun, a divine literature.

It is also true that the hand would sometimes go into a factory, start up the conveyor belts and madly assemble amazing gadgets, strange amalgams and marvelous gimmicks, all the while whistling with its strange humour until it fell down, exhausted.

Of all things, the hand most enjoyed slapping the faces of dictators when they made big speeches on television. This made the hand well-known to all despots, but due to the fact that these programs are pre-taped, the mad escaping hand never had the pleasure of having its handiwork seen by the masses. So if you ever see a political speech and, after a commercial, the great leader comes back on looking a little stunned, a widening red imprint spreading out on his cheeks, look at that shape, that map, that message in the right light and you will see it for what it really is — the mark of a mad hand.

# THE ESCAPED COCK

For a long time the escaped cock worked in a Welfare office gathering contempt for humanity. Dressed in a hat, it learned to speak in a deep voice, practising by saying "No, no, no, no, no, no, no!" over and over again. At night the cock would go home and deflate. It would lie around limp on its bed, curled up like a huge worm dreaming of power and smelling of Aqua Velva. The cock could not accept that it had no bones — that it was just blind flesh. Desperately, the cock began to don new disguises and wander. The cock in Washington. The cock hanging around outside gun stores. The cock eating human food — meat, meat, meat. For a while the cock wore a dress and pretended to be a woman, but the cock wanted to know about murder so it joined the army. It volunteered for firing squads whenever it could and so came to shoot human being after human being until it no longer felt anything about them — shooting them through the heart, shooting them in the mind, shooting and shooting and shooting. As time went by, the cock began to rise through the ranks from soldier to sergeant to major. A general! Always a loner. Four stars — a sham, an inhuman thing, an alien presence in the army. But now the cock could get close to the bombs, the great fertile bombs, bombs like eggs in underground ranks. The cock had the power. It could rub its face on the bombs, mad about having no bones, a little crazy, bursting at odd times into tears, but a good soldier. Not so good on TV though. The face twitched. What if they uncovered the awful truth? This was no human being. This was an awful escaped cock. This was the big, violent dick, the maniac genital. This was the terrifying schizophrenic cock — the killer cock of the world. There was a tense moment when the cock was asked its first question: "Now tell us, General Le Coq, to your knowledge was the army in any way involved?" The cock took a hanky and wiped some sweat from its glans. Then it spoke in its deepest voice, "No, no, no, no, no, no, no!"

# THE MAN WITH THE NITROGLYCERIN TEARS

The man with the nitroglycerin tears, his sorrow terribly intact, stared from a window and waited for rain. It was amazing how much pain he kept bottled up in blue and white eyes — thick, compressed pain, like sap, colouring his features in deep rings of rage, spreading out like poison to the rim of his fingertips. If the trees were this full of pain, they would twist in agony, making hideous shapes over graveyards, screaming with the wind, black howls from hell on earth. Aaaaah, the pain that would not leak out of his eyes. How this pain thickened in his throat, the hands grasping like roots in his sleep, mad, in a frenzy to be caught up in something. Perhaps he would fly and weep in an airplane, the bright explosions of his tears like bombs in the night below. Weep over barracks, weep over parliaments. Weep, sobbing with grief over churches and educational institutes. For so long he had hidden those nitroglycerin tears in the pockets of his eyes he was dreaming through them, fantastic griefs. He thought of his mother, of children. He thought of love he could not be reached by and imagined midnight arms factories lighting up the dark skies with his aerial grief. One morning he woke up, and as though coming through the high dome of a cathedral, the sunlight streamed in through a large tear which had somehow escaped during the night and now lay quivering, explosively, on his cheek. For hours he lay there, tilting his head back without blinking, letting gravity slowly draw the tear back into his eye, hardly daring to breathe lest he explode.

One day in the street, like a great wave, it finally overcame him. He sobbed, bent over and watched as the first two great luminous teardrops hurtled down to the pavement. As he wept, louder and louder, the man was blown apart, sizzled, ruptured, burnt by grief, saying "Aaaaah children, children, children. My babes, my babes."

Only a few pieces of the man with the nitroglycerin tears were found — an eyelid in Kenora, an arm in Minsk, a lot of blood in Lake Erie, and in various parts of Northern Ontario, small red pieces of his heart. These were gathered up and put to rest beneath a stone which read, "Here lies the man with the nitroglycerin tears. Of all things in life, he loved rain best."

# THE MAN WHO BROKE OUT OF THE LETTER X

Once, while the soldiers were asleep, a man broke out of the letter X. He burst through its centre and emerged into the world in a loincloth and began to run. He was past the soldiers before they could see him, and when they did see him, they just stood there rubbing their eyes and wondering if he was real. The man ran through the winding streets of the city faster and faster in apparent terror and many people saw him as he darted here and there along the cobblestones. As the day progressed and the streets contained more and more people, the man who had broken out of the letter X would suddenly find himself face to face with a pedestrian. When this happened his terror would redouble and he would dart off even quicker, shrieking as he continued his flight. Soon the news spread that a man had broken out of the letter X and there began to be a great deal of apprehension about him. Where had he come from? What did he want? Why did he flee from them as though they were monsters? The governor approved the order and helicopters were sent to follow the running man. Faster and faster he ran, his lungs burning up, coughing as he scrambled and fled across the plains and plazas of that immense city. Cars screeched to a halt, crowds gasped as he passed. As the police began to close in, the man was like a tiger in the jungle, scrambling up walls, leaping up stairs, jumping over the canyons between small buildings. They caught him at last in a net. A very beautiful man — a man as beautiful as they had ever seen. But when the flashbulbs went off and he looked into the faces of his captors, he let out shrieks of horror which were like nothing they had ever heard before. As he screamed, the man went into a spasm — his back arched under him, his jaw clicked open, his eyes bulged, and all of him trembled like a leaf of death. And so he died, this man who had broken out of the letter X. And why he came here and what he was running from no one ever knew, but from then on the soldiers guarded the letter X with greater vigilance, so that if anyone else broke out they could send him back inside for his own good.

# THE WISE MAN

This is the story of the wise man who lived in a pit instead of up on a mountain. And when he wanted to talk to his God, he looked down at the earth instead of up into the sky. When he slept, he hung upside down from a device in straps facing the ground. You see, he had spotted a star in the centre of the earth. It was a dark star of soil and soot and blood and it was to this dark thing that he uttered down his prayers. The sun seemed like a darker force upon this wise man. He worshipped the frozen star in the ground, the white star of permafrost beneath the magma and the robe of char. What a glowing spiritual star it was for him. A bogus heaven, of course — a small device to let the actual implications of paradise slide by. For he would be helpless if he had to think about paradise. It was like grease — this ersatz heaven in the depths of his soily sky, and each worm, each bug and mole, a mysterious dweller in the heights, a burrowing angel.

Pursuing this unusual course, the wise man found a way of writing which would absolutely destroy his thoughts. Next he discovered a way of singing which was a worse fate for a song than absolute silence. Wiser and wiser he grew as he forgot. Finally, the wise man devised a method for communicating which destroyed all telepathy and understanding. It was a very clever and necessary device that he hoped would do away altogether with the dangers of talking.

When the populace finally discovered the antics of this wise man they were at first frightened and then outraged. Gathered into a mob and stirred by their leaders, they went to get him, a cold autumn of hands falling on his naked flesh. What a torment it was for him to be touched and turned upright at last. Chanting hosannas, they carried this colossal wise man up to the mountain peak. They held him aloft for seven days on a pole as he mumbled and chattered, destroying his feelings with poetry, ruining his desperate prayers with speech. At last they shoved him into a rocket, laughing cruelly as the vehicle blasted off.

Helplessly he wept in the dark as the rocket dug deeper and deeper into the darkness of the sky, further and further from the mighty tug of his earth-star. Just before he went mad his hands floated up over his head in the weightlessness and he began to scream in the language no one understands.

## POINTS

A man had a job putting the points back on old arguments. When, for instance, a particularly aged theory had been rather obviously blunted by some more modern, more aptly pointed enemy, he could, in a brew of well-steeped opinions, philosophies, religions, apostrophes, and semantics, restore the point somewhat. Knowing this I took him my old ragged love, the one whose piercing had ceased to move even me. I showed him this poor, blunted, unlucky love of mine and he said, "O this one is easy," and began to mix up a batch of old poetry and high romance. When he had steeped it to a froth, he thrust my old utterly pointless love into it and waited. Finding on withdrawal that it was still blunt, he held it for a while, puzzled, over a fire made from the desires of many thirsty men in deserts. Then he hammered it with a metal made of loneliness. With a knife of empty nights he hacked. But still it remained intolerably, impenetrably dull and blunted, so he returned it to me. "A man's love," he said, "must be as pointed as his tongue. It must have the same direction as his hands and mouth. It must pierce all distances and agonies, overcome all enemies. Yours obviously is of an inferior quality. It hasn't even stood the ardours of your poor little life. Pity humanity if this is the one strong thing that comes from it." Thus chided, I went outside jingling the cash in my pockets. "At last!" I said to myself. "At last I am ready for business."

# THE MAN WHO THOUGHT A WOMAN WAS GOD

There was a man who saw a woman walking in front of him and he had a very intense "feeling" that she was God, come to walk on earth, this time as a woman. "I am God, God, God!" she seemed to say with her walk, all the power of Yahweh in her supple limbs, her confident stride. Foolishly the man began following her, unable for the moment to figure out anything else to do. He wanted to look in her eyes. Just to make sure. He would know Yahweh if he looked him in the eyes, but how would he do it? Perhaps he could suddenly accelerate, walk right past her without looking and then somewhere up ahead, stop, stare for a while in a shop window and then, turning, catch her eye as she caught up and passed. No, that was too obvious. And what if it was God? Yahweh would know just what he was up to and quite possibly crush him forever in the mighty fists of his beauty — lay waste to his spirit with a stare of such naked sensuality and power that even the immortal soul-bit would be melted, dazzled out of existence. Then again if he didn't look, he would never know, and he had never had such a strong feeling before.

With the equivalent of a herd of butterflies flapping away in this man's feathery breast, the thought-shots of sunlight broke through him. Aaaaah, a world that had lately seemed so dull and lifeless, bloated by cruelty and submission — now there was possibility in everything. God had come again — this time as a beautiful woman. Well, it was worth dying for then. It was worth having the spirit go up like so much star-stuff and be forever beamed out across the time-space. He must look. Immediately he deked over on a side street and dashed up a parallel road, hardly able to stop a great leap from overcoming him, galloping like a horse, like a ballet dancer. Zoom, he shot past the next intersection with a most incredible intensity, his face pointed unconsciously toward the least stress in the atmosphere, jet-like. Faster and faster he sprinted past the next intersection too, his face like an Aztec airplane. God! He was gonna look God in the eyes and explode! Completely in focus, hardly out of breath, he came to the next corner, stopped, and then slowly sauntered back over to the street God was on, his heart flapping like a rag in the wind. His blood like burning dust.

There, his head enormous, like a cracking planet in his hat, he began to walk back down the original street, just as a bus went by. But where was she? He couldn't see her anywhere. "She's not in any of these stores. Nor these doorways. Nor . . . No! It can't be!" The heart squirting a cold gush up against the throat. "Break! Break! You strip of ice, you cry-keeper. Burst open O shattered breast of bells and trumpets, for she was on that bus." And that bus was gone. He had lost her.

# THE UNCATCHABLE MAN

There was once an uncatchable man and nothing could catch this man, not traps, not houses, not colds, not people with nets, nothing could catch him because he was free and easy and he couldn't be nailed down. He just traveled around in search of a special jewel he was after, and would slip out of any sticky situation with a high squeal and some very fine rolling. Eventually the uncatchable man found his way to a certain pollen patch, and being very white, he decided to roll there, taking on for a while the fabulous rainbow hues of nature. While he was rolling there, rolling and laughing about how easily he had always evaded capture, the resident butterfly came by and asked him, "How are you liking the trap?" "What do you mean 'the trap?'" he asked. "The trap you're in," the butterfly replied. "You are caught in a butterfly trap." "Ah-ha-ha!" the man laughed, for he knew the butterfly was wrong and that nothing could catch him. "Well why don't you leave then?" the butterfly asked. "I could leave if I wanted to," the man yelled, continuing to roll — rolling, if anything, more joyfully and laughing louder and louder as he moved deeper and deeper into the pollen trap. Rolling and laughing and thinking about how much capture he had evaded and chortling with shrill glee. "Bet you can't get away now," the butterfly screamed above him. "Bet you like the trap now!" "O how I love the trap!" the man yelled. "I love the trap — so much fun to get away from. So much fun to roll like this, right up to the stickiest flowers themselves and then run away." Saying this, the man pointed to the bent-down lips of a huge pollen-swollen flower which was at the very heart of the trap. "Aaaaah, what a sweet flower!" he said in a high hysterical voice, observing with great appetite the sticky climb of pollen higher up the blue and red and purple petals. Suddenly he felt a great urge to stick his face right up one of the large floral bells. "Watch this," he said to the butterfly, and getting down on his multi-coloured knees and folding back his pollen-smeared wings he ducked his head down under, right up into the open mouth of it. "O sweet, sweet sticky colours!" the man giggled from within, letting the multi-coloured syrups ooze down onto his shoulders and draw him in. "O sweet and tasty flower!" he bellowed. And then of course, just as it looked like he had been captured, he popped out with a shriek of triumph, jumping up and down mockingly in front of the butterfly. "Well, bye-bye butterfly," he said, turning his back on her as he ran across the pollen patch and out into the world. Bitterly, the butterfly watched the uncatchable man go running, and then she returned, weeping, to her nest at the top of the flowers. Someday her tender blossoms would be restored. Someday she would catch a mate. Sadly, sadly as the moonlight fell and the great whoops and shrieks of laughter of the uncatchable man faded into the starlight and dew, the tears of the butterfly dripped down the stalks of her flowers and formed, for an instant, a jewel — the very jewel which the uncatchable man is, even now, frantically searching for.

# POET'S PROGRESS

I. Thanks to a short, squat frame and an early effort at weight-lifting, this big poet is able to carry about the huge "I" which various sages have awarded him. And to his credit it should be said that even though it would often be much easier to carry it sideways, he always carries it straight up lest it be mistaken for a hyphen. It is said that this huge "I" weighs over 40 kilos and, being made of certain inferior metals, is known to give off a radiation of intense arrogance. Observing the strain and general distortion of his features which the support of this huge "I" has cost this poet, one has to marvel again at the strength and beautiful fortitude of those other poets whose task it is to carry around the entire word "Important."


II. What his head did made an elastic hat necessary. All day he stuffed himself with pig and potato and cow pieces and his head grew bigger and bigger. It was gigantic by the time his hat popped off with a snap at night and sent him into his "poetic" frenzy. For then, discarnate, like a demon at large, he would twist and writhe in the air, all the time mumbling and expostulating with a pompous air into a tape recorder. Afterward, when his fingers began to soften, when at last he could see what was left of his feet, he would proudly let go the last of his excess wind by saying the word "Penultimate."

# HIT SONGS FROM HEAVEN

It is snowing the freedom pamphlets of heaven. Sheet music from the angel factories. Hit songs are flying by in the breeze, each one written on a giant snowflake. Hit songs from heaven and if the pianists can only catch one on a music stand cold enough, we shall hear at last the wildest tinkles of angelic composers. What a list, what a reel the high music of heaven has! Such snaps, such snags, such hooks! It is snowing the divine anthems of heaven and to hear but the few choice phrases my magnificent instrument can utter before I go wild myself will send you all into reveries, passions, fuckeries, and adorations. You will want to leap and dance in the streets, burning great characters of the alphabet in joyous exaltation. Come and hear my crazy Chopin — nine bars of your angelic attitude — before these great overtures are lost upon my body heat, ravished of their writings as surely as pages in a furnace.

## SULTAN OF THE SNOWFLAKES

Because his footprints are constantly changed by gimmickry and magic, a particularly unique beast is hired by the snow-makers to run on the spot all day, while sheaves of snow are rapidly stamped and moved on by industry beneath him. He is something like a creative elephant — a heavenly pachyderm whose divine bellowings of joy are sometimes used to puff out a great flag in that place. Stomp, stomp he goes and the snowflakes, with the thrust he gives them, fall from the firmament, filling up the kennels and the dreams and the beggar's cup full of snow, so that all might be cast down together on designated days. He regards the snowflake as propaganda for Utopia — each one, if you could read it, would tell of swamps he walked in singing, of prehistoric moons and governments of love. Stomp, stomp he goes — the immortal pamphleteer whom children read on fingertips with wonder. "I will change the world," he says, "just before the melt." Summertimes he goes on holiday, is called "Sultan of the Snowflakes," and for a hobby spends days and days designing the faces of beautiful women.

# EGO-ANGELS

Ego-angels live on in bandshells long after their legal time on earth. There, if they like, they can conduct again any fanfare or all the fanfares. And so they grow bigger and bigger in their bandshells until the music is too small for them and they must float up at last to their redemption. When ego-angels come at last into Paradise, they are welcomed by a legion of a billion crazed ego-angels blowing the titanic fanfares of all the religions. Then they get the bad news — no, they cannot immediately begin conducting the fanfares of Paradise. They must wait their turn. And so it is said that the grip of ego-angels upon bandshells becomes more and more desperate and the earthly fanfares closer and closer to those of heaven.

## QUIET CAPS

Across the nation our wizards wear quiet caps and learn in silence: geographies, histories, and tales of old. So fragile are these pointed caps that one single trumpet blast could shatter them. A pin dropping would ravish them utterly, and like destarched flowers they would wither and fall about their eyes. And so the wizards keep their babies in exquisite nurseries below and above the ground, for imagine what libraries the screech of a baby might consume. Imagine what mathematics, medicine, and poetries might be lost if the children were allowed to frolic. So, wise in the ways of sedimentary rock, full of famous dates and high gibberish, our wizards bring their children up from underground at night for lullabies. For a brief time, as our wizards sing, those delicate hats glow in the dusk. Then, as the moon rises and the children sleep, being used up, they are consumed into dust.

# WANT THE WATER!

All those stones you threw when you were in school — they come back to you when you are drowning. That is when they hang around your neck like the lards of the rich. But I have dispensed with my advice about water. People will not hoard it as they do gold. Nor when they are unnaturally hungry will they drink it excessively. Perhaps they do not want the rainbows coalescing in their blood. They run to something like food or a fuck and then complain about dissatisfaction. Long for the water, I warned. Want nothing else more badly than the big silver thing or it will be your undoing. But they walked by me, fat with albatross and tank passes. There was nothing I could do; even I had the corpse slippers. Soon the water was everywhere wasted. It lapped in hungrily, obsessively, shore to shore like a tongue at teeth. There wasn't a single place it didn't want to get into. It knocked even on the door of the invisible air, but at last all the palaces were locked to it and it had only those terrible systems of sewers — the cities and the souls — the incredible veins of everything human to dance in. And that is when it remembered again the idea of rain. Now again all those crowns I threw away, the great robes of water, the swirling aqua-diem in the fish bowl — they all come back to me. I who am not satisfied with the oceans and oceans of it. I who am still thirsty in the torrent, screaming more and more. I sing to you one last time about the heaviness of gold for astral travelers, and that gravity persists even underground.

# BOOK 5
# COMIX

## CURLY'S REPORT

I could never speak about it before because nothing had ever been said to make me think anything positive could come of it. So I would try to make it funny and people actually laughed. But Moe was really hitting me. He *was* poking me in the eyes. He *was* twisting my ear right 'round in circles and everybody just watched and laughed. Is the horrifying hollow clunk of one head colliding with another funny, even if you go "wooo"? I should have let my needs be known. I should have said, "This isn't funny, I'm hurting!" But I couldn't speak. And Moe was kicking me hard a lot of the time — kicking me in the coccyx or tugging on my tongue. And when I wasn't tensing up against the next onslaught, I was watching poor, sweet Larry getting his hair torn out in fistfulls that sounded like sheets of cotton ripping. The poor bastard — poked, seared, scalded, torn. Sure, I hated Moe — more than anything. And yes, it's true, whether deliberately or not I still don't know, 'cause I may have just convinced myself it was an accident, but one day Moe got his head completely stuck in a stovepipe and me and Larry decided we were gonna "help" him. So, well, we put our feet on his shoulders and pulled at the stovepipe as hard as we both could. After a while, when he stopped screaming in there, all you heard were these "pingy" sounds of his neck bones popping and we knew we could just tug his head right off if we wanted. But we stopped and tried to twist the stovepipe off instead. Once again he gasped and cried out, but we just went right on with both hands, turning that stovepipe 'round and 'round till his nose bone crunched and steam shot out. But those day are gone now. People thought it was funny, so we went along with it. Now we pay. And that's just the way it is.

# WITNESS REPORT

Well the little one — Moe, the nasty one — when he found out what had happened, he got so enraged, he deliberately poked two fingers right into Curly's eyes. I've never seen a man poked in the eyes before and I was quite shocked. Curly, in agony, pulled both palms down over his face to his chin, one hand after the other, in rapid succession, all the while emitting an agonized kind of "wub-wub-wub-wub" sound, high in register, dog-like in intensity. I watched helplessly as the same arm which had so cruelly poked the fingers into Curly's eyes shot back, the elbow high, right onto the bridge of Larry's nose. This caused Larry to do something which deeply disturbed me. Taking the huge monkey wrench he had been holding, he somehow managed to spike its grips up Moe's nostrils, and with some quick turns, to tighten it to grip the septum. To my horror, while Curly inscribed a heel-driven circle on the floor and continued his heart rending "wub-wub-wubs," Larry proceeded to twist Moe's nose completely around on his face until the cartilage yielded a sharp "pop." Unable to move, Moe began to run on the spot, going "Nya-aaa-aaaa!" in agony.

# WITNESS REPORT II

Perhaps the most horrifying part of it all, though, is the terrible and unexpected sounds human body parts make as they are yanked, disconnected, and pierced. For, unlike the muffled under-flesh retorts we would expect from snapping femurs and popping joints, we get highly oscillating "Proing!"-type sounds, more reminiscent of the mechanical world: springs, gaskets, etc. Human flesh, when whacked, sounds much more like wood than water, for instance, and there are apparently notches in the neck that creak in precise increments when corkscrewed: "Nok! Nok! Nok!" till the face comes right back 'round again, ready to be let go. And these are only a few of the many violent and repetitively brutal, even handicapping acts which I saw these three men perform during my three-week stay. The surprising thing to me, though, was the speed at which they reconciled. After repeated brutal assaults they could apparently, without ceremony or apology, completely forgive, forget, and get along with one another. (If only to perform one more foolish, useless task.) More than their own violence, however, was called into play. They had an enormous propensity for attracting and eliciting aggression from those around them. Perhaps the most humiliating thing that can be done to a human being is to shove a cream pie in his or her face. When such an attack occurs in a room full of people and pies, these three men have a strange catalytic, chain reaction effect on even the most distinguished guests. One can barely watch when all, finally, give way — the good and the bad, the handsome and the sad — to this profoundly humiliating urge to throw a pie. To see heads jerked back by pies, heads shoved down, suffocatingly deep into pies. To see pies splat two, three people at a time. To see people shoved headfirst into wedding cakes, and vast vats of icing dumped on heaps of rioting people. To watch helplessly as faces, nostril-flared, are forced into foam and cherry, and sense the almost ecstatic quality of these actions is a profoundly disturbing and ultimately unsettling experience, which ought not to be witnessed by the faint of heart.

# THE STOOGE BY-LAWS

It is illegal to poke a stooge in the eye. Falling to the floor and running in a sideways circle is prohibited. There will be no hair-pulling in the common room. Please do not bring pliers into these premises. It is forbidden, while running on the spot, super-fast, to exhale steam from the nostrils. There will be absolutely no pulling out of chunks of hair. No excoriating the eyes. It is wrong to punch the lungs out. Anyone caught laughing at violent acts will be expelled. Until further notice, all pies are strictly forbidden in the cafeteria area. It is a crime to seat a stooge in a catapult. A stooge may not give final unction. No electrocuting stooges. Anyone caught hanging a stooge will be suspended.

# THE THREE DISCIPLE STOOGES

Curiously, the only censored version of the Stooges is the rarely screened "The Three Stooges in Galilee." This episode is rumoured to show Curly in Jerusalem, spending an entire day stealing fish from various merchants. Larry, elsewhere, pilfers loaf after loaf of bread from all the bakeries. Moe, meanwhile, has ingested a magic mushroom of some kind while scarfing the Messiah's abandoned stew. As he stands on the table extemporizing to the gathered masses about lilies and things, Curly and Larry successfully deliver, beneath the table, the loaves and fishes. The miracle is ready. After the sermon, when the bakers and the fishmongers see the banquet that has been prepared for them, they recognize their pilfered wares and rise up to crucify all three.

## MY THREE STOOGES

In the equally rare "My Three Stooges," Moe is a father and Curly and Larry are little kids. And he still beats them! In these episodes it's not dames that Curly's always after — it's Mom. Moe, as in all versions of the Stooges, repeatedly pops both children in the eyes. The sonic effects, however, have been altered. They are squelchier now. A little painful to hear, but still possibly funny. Arse kicks have a little coccyx crack-and-crunch undertone, while the two-in-a-line, double child-face-slap is actually the sound of a wet seal being thwapped by fishermen on a marble floor, twice! Curly and Larry have learned to laugh a lot of the physical stuff off. They are geniuses at turning their shock, the deep sense of betrayal, into big, camera-hogging hams that are truly hilarious. These are great child actors! Because it's the old days, we are not allowed to actually see Moe when he thrashes their asses. He takes them in a room off-camera. And the kids are great. They're trembling great. There's water in their veins. Their bowels are going. Moe is going to beat them. The next time we see them, their asses are in buckets and there is steam rising from them. They have obviously been crying. Curly, even though his voice is hoarse from screaming, manages the first mock "Nyaah ahah," making Larry pull his goo-face. During the filming of this series, Curly Howard, the actor who plays Curly, succumbs to a stroke and is unable to perform. But Curly is replaced by older brother Shemp. Shemp dies, also of a stroke. The final Stooge is Joe Besser. Joe takes on the moniker "Curly Joe," and keeps the part until the show is cancelled due to poor ratings.

# THE THREE SEXUAL SURVIVOR STOOGES

In a bizarre twist, we have uncovered a case of Stooge sexual abuse. And it's *still* funny. In this series, instead of poking Curly in the eyes, the aptly named Moe gives him rapid pokes up the asshole. Larry suffers repeated penis yanks, twists, scrunches, whacks, and hammers. All with extremely unexpected sonic repercussions. "Doing! Dwang! Floompf!" Larry's penis is cut, burnt, yanked, or twisted off an average of seven times an episode. Fortunately for Larry, his penis seems to have more regenerative properties than Wolverine. Ever-reborn and newly sensitive, Larry is an immortal abuse victim. And it's *still* funny. In the episode with the elephant, Curly, Larry, and Moe have all been locked, bare-bummed, into stocks. When the elephant sees the large pot of Vaseline, it fucks each of the Stooges with a big, popping, tearing sound. Moe as usual moans "Nyaaaa aaaaah!", while Curly goes "Wooo wooo wooo." And it's *still* funny!

# BLADERUNNER STOOGES

In this episode, Moe is an android doomed to die. His hair has only just started to fall out. It is a young Moe, more handsome than we would have thought possible. He has seen the cargo ships on fire off Orion. He has seen things you've never dreamed, but now, at his peak, he must die. It's part of his programming — unless he can find Curly and Larry. Curly and Larry invented Moe. And a million more Moes. Moes everywhere all over the stars like little lumberjacks building the brick shit-house of interstellar commerce. And what if some of these android-Moes should get ambitious or go crazy? Well that's why they had the built-in time limit thing. It was written into the materials of their genesis. It *is* them — this early death. How Moe hates it. How enraged he is at these little men who have made him. Who are less than him. In the end he finds Curly and Larry but they assure him haughtily that he is untreatable. They make offensive platitude-like remarks drawn largely from self-help books they have only just read and therefore believe. Moe says, "Pick two fingers." Curly stupidly complies. Moe rapidly pokes them in Curly's sockets, deep past his eyeballs, into the soft brain stuff behind. Too-red blood runs out. Moe turns to Larry and says, "Pick two fingers."

# THE IMMORTAL STOOGES

Due to some Satanic deals, no one at this particular banquet can actually be killed. They can, however, be maimed, exploded, and pierced. So Moe pulls out the double-barreled twelve gauge shotgun and says, "Hey Larry, take a look in the binoculars." Moe's gone a bit far this time. He lets Larry have it, full blast, in both eyes, basically disintegrating the top two-thirds of Larry's head. Some of the slushy, pink stuff still caught, hangs from the remaining hair, flip-top-box-like. Larry, unable to see, lets Moe have it in the guts. Unfortunately, it's not Moe. It's the fat diplomat who has just bent down to bow to the finicky lady. This gentleman is outraged when his buttocks are blasted open. En masse, his seven sons open fire on the Stooges. Unfortunately, they are terrible marksmen. Curly is going "Wooo Wooo" as fast as possible. He has been sped up or something. He has transformed the gunshots into bells and buzzers as he dekes and ducks, still expertly pulling faces. Moe, however, is being rammed again and again against the blood-spattered walls as he is repeatedly shot by the brothers. Each time, he rises back up more and more raggedly. Unfortunately, so does the small boy who has been putting glass in the punch. So does the overly dignified lady in the green lamé gown. Now several comedians pull out really big hand cannons and, laughing wildly, begin to blow away as many heads as possible, exploding them like watermelons. Guns are coming out everywhere; exploded, wounded, immortal people are shooting wildly — everyone's being drawn in. The whole place is just strings of guts and guns, implacably engaged in hatred and rage. Only Curly still dodges the inaccurates. Only Curly — immaculate, unkillable, and still funny.

## CURLY, LARRY, AND OSWALD

In this episode it is Curly who rides beside Jackie in the Cadillac on that fateful day. Instead of sitting back in a dignified way, however, Curly is standing and cupping his hands high in the air over his head while people cheer. As the car turns into Dealey Plaza and the bullets strike, there is a sudden piercing sound of school bells and big chunks of Curly's head come flying off. Curly, who has been knocked ass-over-tips right off the back of the Cadillac, gets up from the bloody mess he's in and starts running around, trying to find bits of his brains, while Larry and Moe conduct an investigation. Afterward, Curly, who is immortal in this episode, is put in a box and never let out.

# THE PRESLEY TWINS

It is widely known that Elvis was a twin. Official documents tell us that Elvis' identical twin brother, Caan, died at birth. But baby Caan never really died. There were always two Presley boys. When one appeared the other disappeared. When one emerged the other hid. Mrs. Presley liked it that way. A kid in the closet and a kid on TV. Usually, it was Caan who was kept in the closet; but when Caan came out Elvis went in, and that's how it was from day one, for God had sent the two down and no one else knew but Vernon and Lou. Elvis had the raspy voice, the one that sang "Jailhouse Rock," the one that sang "Hound Dog" — that hacksaw thing in the throat. Then he would leave the stage and Caan would come on and do the "Love Me Tenders," the "Don't Be Cruels" in a sweet, milky voice and no one knew. No one knew but Vernon and Lou and no one ever suspected. After the fame came, Caan started to want to come out of the closet but Mother wouldn't allow it. There were threats, scenes. The brothers started fighting. Then, when he was drafted, it was Elvis who did all the time while Caan slacked off. This was when Caan started doing prescription drugs — all the pharmaceuticals he could get his hands on. You see, Lou was the Doc and the Doc knew, and he thought he was prescribing for two but Caan was scarfing the lot. The twins began to look different. That is why, after the army, Caan and Elvis did so little TV. There is a moment in the Elvis *Live from Hawaii* video, though, that is very telling. You think it's live and uncut but those who saw the original remember "Elvis," after sleazing his way through "Love Me Tender," asking to be excused. He gets up laughing and leaves the whole world hanging for four minutes as he goes to the washroom. What is now evident is that the real Elvis was in there wearing an identical outfit. He came out and did that great hacksaw vocal on "One Night With You." This is Elvis at his best. He can't stop smiling. There is no self-deprecation now. But notice his right hand; the familiar knuckleduster is no longer present — one of the few times any small detail of the elaborate substitution becomes detectable on camera. After that, there began to be more and more physical differences between the two men. Sometimes Elvis would start a gig thin and confident, then Caan would do the second night, already starting to bulge. The cheap American pharmaceuticals had begun to break down his capillaries. Elvis withdrew and watched helplessly from the sidelines as his brother slipped into the puffy, pathetic narcosis of the famed last days. The man who died on the toilet that day — his body should never have been found. He was to have been discreetly buried, out of the way finally, so that Elvis the survivor might emerge at last: miraculously thin, confident, pelvic, and laughing, to conduct the greatest comeback of all time. But the body *was* found. And to all the world this was Elvis. Stricken with the loss of his brother, the real Elvis saw his chance at freedom. Without telling a soul, he headed for the nearest shopping plaza. And that is why there are so many sightings. Do you really think that many people could be wrong? It is Elvis that they are seeing. He is out there. Still.

# PARALLELVIS UNIVERSE 2003

Saddam demands the U.S. turn over Elvis Presley. The U.S. says "No, we couldn't, even if we wanted to. Elvis is no more. Elvis died." But the Iraqis claim they have numerous reports from defectors. It is well known — Elvis has been seen at supermarkets. Not just Elvis, but numerous Elvises. A proliferation of Elvises, unstable, explosive. If Elvis is unleashed again the effect on the masses will be destructive. They demand the turn-over of Elvis or they will attack. It is asserted repeatedly that Elvis died of a heart attack on August 16th, 1977. The U.S. provides documents: death certificates, coroners' reports, photos, but they are disbelieved, mocked as forgeries. The United Nations confirms there has been absolutely no sign of the living Elvis for years. Reports of there being a still-living Elvis are considered to be mass fantasies thought up by freaks. Wouldn't he have told his own daughter, Lisa Marie? They send a team to look for Elvis. They interview Sam Phillips. Still no Elvis. But, they say, that's just because people are afraid to tell them where Elvis is. Finally, despite world protest, the Iraqi army comes up from Mexico, immediately securing the Texas oil fields. They quickly conquer America, but when the dust settles neither Elvis nor Bush is anywhere to be found. The American people are very thirsty; their water supply has been shut off by the war. Their children have been murdered. It's reported that Iraq deliberately lied about Elvis being alive. "It wasn't just about Elvis, anyway," says Saddam. "George Bush was evil. He was never democratically elected. He executed more people in the state of Texas than all the other states combined." They leak stories about the Nazi past of Bush's ancestry. Everybody agrees that America does seem a lot more relaxed now that Bush is gone. Anyway, the capture of Elvis is considered imminent. There is a report that Elvis is likely in Canada. Canada denies having Elvis. Iraq warns Canada that they will treat harbouring Elvis as an act of war. Saddam makes a big speech, saying that the U.S.A., Canada, and Britain are part of an "Axis of Elvis."

## THE NEW CRUISE MAN

He walks in calmly over the mountains, at first very wooden, but then more and more smoothly as he goes down a prescribed road to a prescribed city, and there, with a wide radium glow in his eyes, he joins in polite cocktail conversation, waiting for someone to say the word "orange."

# THE COMBINATION CRUISE MAN AND WOMAN

Both of them have been given a very strong impression of a location. It is usually an embassy or a beautiful public statue or garden. Coming from different directions to this spot, a tug greater than that of the atom bomb to Nagasaki will draw them together. They will veer in, arms flailing helplessly toward each other like dead cracking planets, a deep sonic boom when their hands touch. Then, the real threat being their ensuing exhibitionism, they will begin to perform slow, persuasive, public foreplay. Eventually, after much musical, but overtly sexual dancing and rubbing up against one another, he will draw first one, then another, of her black stockings down. There, on one knee, with a smooth upward swooping of his gold-dust hands he will stroke her breasts as he rubs his tongue into her nucleonic heat. Not till his big, atomic, techno-gristle, all glowing and red, finally pops out with a tear from his flannels, will people finally begin to shout at them. But by then it will be too late. She will arch over backward; he will insert the big black dinger into her glowing crack. And when the first zero flickers in the egg's eye, the whole locale goes up like the wings of a thousand thrushes.

# THE SURREALIST AIR FORCE

For some reason the item in the universe most amenable to long-distance accuracy is the pig. A two-tonne pig, when it is hurled from the sky, breaks open in a great gush. That's why we are dropping the pigs, dropping the pigs. All our swine production goes into this. No one eats bacon. Every drop of pig's blood is for your country. A man loves his pig but it's just a bag of blood for the war effort. We need your pig! One of millions to drop squealing. But then a two-tonne pig hits a mosque. The entire Arab world is outraged. It has been claimed that the pigs were strategic, accurate, state of the art. But an entire neighbourhood is killed by falling pigs. They threaten to drop Cher. There is a massive protest. All around the world people march to stop them from dropping Cher. They say, "No decisions have yet been made about dropping Cher." Then they drop Cher. She falls screaming, "If I could turn back time." They threaten to drop Madonna. There are suggestions they may drop Mariah Carey. She will fall doing the high note. They are dropping comedians over glass houses now. How they shriek. How they wail. We are losing at least a celebrity a day to this insane war. All you have to do is hand over Elvis and we will go away. We have the right to protect ourselves from Elvis. They drop blue fish, spring-loaded bibles to nip our nuts. To snap our vaginas shut. They drop broken clocks, blood magnets, poisoned crosses, Pope hats with fire alarms. Down with the elephants. The whales. How the mighty tigers fall, those great claws useless in the naked air. How the jellyfish sail. How the household dogs plummet. From a mile up, a falling cat can kill. Babies — burst open, limbs askew, broken on the barricades, spattered on the training places, smeared on tanks — 5000 bombers, a thousand times a day, so that no area of the city is left untouched. So that the sky is never empty of falling babies. Babies away! Pre-frozen babies never touched but for this one shove. Stiff blue babies who bang like bells and split open in agony when they hit the ground. Starved babies with explosions in their eyes. We are dropping the preemies. Missiles full of quints. Launching the sextuplets. But we're falling behind in baby production. We are fucking like mad trying to keep up with the bloodbath. We need more babies. Have you considered having a baby? Uncle Spam needs you — to have a baby.

## ORDNANCE IN SODOM

Do not pick up the sticky bibles. If one hand gets stuck, do not try to remove with the other or you'll have two hands stuck. If you're already in this predicament do not try to pry yourself away with your heel or your heel will also get stuck. If you are flexible you must not do what the stupidest do — try with your final foot to push yourself off the sticky bible. Otherwise, they will find you like that when they come to harvest the casualties. Stuck like a wolf in a trap. A rare few have even managed to get their faces close enough to the sticky bible to attempt a chin-push. These poor yogis are attached at five points — a most excruciating position to endure for any length of time. Especially in Sodom.

# WMDs

What Massive Deception! What Malevolent Drivel! What Malignant Dogma! Whoosh More Doom! Whack More Disease! We Make Death — Watch Many Die. Weeping, Mourning, Dread. World Mass Disgust. Way More Divided. Way More Debt. Way More Destruction. Wasted Murdered Detainees. Wild Manic Denials. Women Mowed Down Won't Make Democracy. Wanted More Draftees!

# THE EXECUTION OF MALNUTRITION

They took Malnutrition out. They put it up against a wall and shot it. A billion bullets as it bucked and jolted, taking on a different shape with each blast: bird, star, stone, old man, woman, child, child, child. They riddled Malnutrition remorselessly but there was no killing it. Not the fire, not disease, not the explosion of hunger, not the haunted faces of billions could end its life. Malnutrition just took them on and stood there, wide-eyed and staring, its long overdue ticket to the banquet, its death warrant still clutched in its infant fist.

# HATING OUR CHILDREN

Yes, our children incense us. We fall to the floor screaming at them, we sputter and shriek. Words fail us. We want to beat them all the time. Put them into corners. Cane their buttocks. Burn their hands. We want to slap their faces all day. But none of this is really legal. We have to work within the system. Hence the corporations which have given us superb technologies for poisoning the soil. For torturing the trees of the neighbourhood and killing off the atmosphere. Thank you, elected officials, for this great leap forward in achieving our revenge against our children and our children's children. Our hate reaches on, seven generations long. We've worked out how to get the most for us and leave the least for them. How delicious, then, to take them out for a joyride in the chief weapon we are using against them — the car. Snickering at their happy faces, knowing that every mile eats up another minute. We feed them the hunger. Eagerly we pour them libations of liquid thirst. We betray them with kisses. Brand them in weird rituals, snip their foreskins. And if their poor faces should cause the hate to soften we have circling places, communions of hate where the hate can be strengthened and again made strong. A whole faith of hate that beats the hate into shape for the deeds, the terrible things it must create. Because God is hate. Because a sudden stop of hating might be dangerous. Hate might move at speeds beyond our bodies' will to resist it. All we need is hate. Hate is consciousness. Hate will keep us together — the hate we have for our children.

# THE STARVED MAN

The starved man has always been a popular figure: those familiar eyes huge with suffering, bigger than his belly, his mouth set firm in the sadness. We have always watched the travels of the starved man. The starved man and friends shot one by one in the back of the head, blown over into Cambodian graves. How well he dies, that man — pulled under by the sharks — his old act with the napalm, running screaming into the jungle. No one has ever died in so many places. The starved man goes to India. The starved man in Ethiopia. The adventures of the starved man in Uganda. How the starved man ate dirt. How he was tortured in Chile. The starved man goes to Haiti. No one has ever died as often as the starved man, yet somehow he manages to keep on starving. One day he will be recognized for this great talent of his. One day he will get an award. Ladies and gentlemen, a man you're all familiar with, my good friend, the starved man.

# THE STARVED MAN GOES TO AMERICA

When the starved man came to America, he began clapping his starved hands and chanting. As he was wearing only a diaper, the children followed him and soon all of America walked behind the chanting of the starved man. He led them to their houses and said, "Now, these are your temples." And he took them into the fields and said, "Here are your holy objects, here the sacred seed and the kernel of wheat. Here is the holy corn and the water that is a godhead." He took them into their kitchens, their cupboards and their earth and said, "Here is the paradise, the reward, and the work."

Soon the starved man had walked all over America and the footprints of the people were everywhere. This being accomplished, he stepped back into the ark of pitch and ribs he had come in, and, paddling with his hands, began to make his way out to the horizon with all the eyes of America watching him. Out in the sunset, as it seemed his frail craft would burn up in its light, the starved man blew a kiss and sent it out over the world. The Americans gasped and swooned with love as the kiss landed huge and fiery on their coastline. There was a small hiss and then the whole country, like a silver sheet of gasoline, went up in the inferno of his kiss. All were disintegrated in that kiss — the beautiful kiss of the starved man.

The starved man sailed on. He sailed on full of love until he was much closer to God.

# POETRY RULES OK

At last poetry is in charge. From now on trains won't run unless the word runs. Poem is the switch. If it's not poetic, it's stuck or stopped, nixed in mid-verse. The hearse stalled halfway to the funeral, the nurse freeze-framed in mid course. Poetry is the fifth force. The organizing principle of matter. To its gravity we surrender these dust motes: law, love, trust and — of course — our votes. "Yes, Poetry rules ok" we say. "Poetry is power." But Plato interrupts, "Doesn't power corrupt?"

So why were we surprised? Ideals are always compromised. But a deconstructionist in charge of housing? Is that wise? Then we had a dada foreign war to pay for: a surrealist air force, clear financial suicide! And now this new constitution of constraint — with just the vowel "I"? No wonder the dictionary's been privatized. The word as cash: their new battle cry — slash. Modifiers/slash, articles/slash, apparatus of the sentence/slash/slash. Does that make sense? And now the scandals. The sonneteer claims innocence. But really, fourteen "gifts" to fourteen "men" fourteen times? And the fifteenth — a man named Mr. Orange — the minister of Rhymes, has just declared the penal code defunct for "lacking assonance." So much for crime. I think you get the grift. Poetry's into poetry. It's self-interest, it's only there to feather its nest. Why, it'll sell the light right out from under those who write and then sit there in the dark, drinking their ink, singing Night? What night?

# PEOPLE WHO LOVE US

People who love us hide in these hills waiting for our passing. They will emerge from the scenery, melt out of the night and accost us with flowers, with small gifts they have shopped for all day. They will walk at us like zombies, their eyes full of kisses they haven't had yet. We have forbidden them to love us. We've made it dangerous to love us but still they come with promises of tenderness. Assurances about tomorrow. People who want to do us good. People who will be devoted to us. People who will do more than half the work. They are always after us and we have to protect ourselves. They are mumbling tales about past lives now, offering to do our laundry. We do our best to keep the lovers away. We have an armoured bus for moving from point to point. Their faces, through its thick windows, are blurry masks, primitive leers. When we get off the bus some of them will be there, waiting for us. Some of them live near our homes. They will have innumerable opportunities to shout poems at us. We might wake up and find one of them weeping in the yard. Some might be building swing sets, cradles, and love seats for us. They have promised to round each other up, but we've noticed they go off kissing and then come back hungrier than ever for our love. We have given them psychiatry gratis; we have returned their importuning with nothing but our honed hate. If we could only stomp out love altogether, then we could be rid of them. But as long as there is love anywhere in the world it is on our doorstep; it is gazing into our windows.

## JESUS AND THE PLUS SIGN

Pontius Pilate said, "Jesus, you are too positive. You push everything toward affirmation, falling never into negativity. You add to the world your gallant and wise soul. You add to the environment your healing walk, your caress of the waters, and to humanity you add some sense of divinity in the flesh, some meaning, some worth. Too damn positive. Add. Add. After I wash my hands and clean my teeth you must carry a huge plus sign up Golgotha so that you can come to know the over-bearing mass of your positivity on the great Mathematics of Rome."

# PSALM 1

God has an endless name. She can never finish writing the cheque. She needs eternity just to identify herself. God's name requires goodness; it needs love to represent itself in nature fully. There must be infinite alphabets. Endless new letters to pick from. New numbers to equate. There must be multifoliate increments of pitch, tone, and colour. To shape just the first great consonant of God's name, we need all the lifetimes we can get, perfecting ourselves for the ultimate diction. Accepting that we are only a small part of one pronouncement. A word that may emerge over generations and still never have begun. God can't just hand you her card. God can't be expected to have a passport. For God there is no "other." No loneliness. Shantih. There are no commandments for God. God listens to all infinity at once. Almost knows who she is. Almost knows us.

# THE NON-VIOLENT BOXER

He came from nowhere. The quickest ducker in the world. The fastest chin in existence. The non-violent boxer, just deking and dodging, while his opponent flails away. *Thwip! Thwip!* Look at that guy move! Look at the way he pops that light bulb-like head straight down, almost as though into some turtle hole in the top of his torso. *Shhzooopp!* And a fist cuts through naked air, the little guy's legs shooting wide apart. Five rounds and he hasn't been touched. If you listen you can hear him over the ring mic trying to persuade his opponent. "Do you think it would be a victory if you beat me?" *Thwip!* "That would be just one more loss for both of us." *Thwip! Thwip!* "The greatest victory of all is in our grasp, but I need you my brother." *Thwip! Thwip! Thwip! Thwip! Thwip!*

# INTERVIEW WITH THE NON-VIOLENT BOXER

How do you account for your win?

"Well, because I am using non-violent techniques I have not only the strength of my body but all the force of truth and history at my disposal. This, coupled with my great agility, is what makes winning possible."

How important is the agility?

"These battles might be fought without the agility but it would be infinitely more painful. I would have to allow myself to be pummeled many times. This would make me less durable as a boxer, and less engaging as an entertainer and artist. My agility is very important."

# BOOK 6
# LOVE AS THOUGH

# THE KISS I JUST MISSED

The kiss I just missed giving you wound up later on another mouth, but by then it had become a little cold and cruel. It wanted to be just burned off in sunbursts and cleansed of its longing. It imparted only melancholy. Where it goes now I don't know. Probably to be used and used on other mouths. Each time, worn down a little more, like a coin, to its true longing. Perhaps it will reach you then from some impartial lover — from some dispassionate goodbye — like a stem cut from its rose. The kiss that didn't make it to your mouth made it instead to Toronto, for I could not be rid of it in Palo Alto. It stained my lips even in Mendocino. In a Triumph Spitfire I could not, by singing out the window, leave a long, burning stream of it hissing in the air. It has become an irreconcilable wound now. A grand comparer. It lands on lips in a regular autumn but it will never be severed from its mouth. I wash it in water — it is there. I wash it in wine — still it is there. Drunken then, singing your name, mouthing it hot and burning into my mind, it has shown me its red edges, its arms and legs that didn't ground. It has talked to me sadly of clothes, of beds it didn't lie down in. What a weeper! It has dragged me under rain. Indelible. Indelible. Wants to go finally to the graveyard of old kisses, each one with its denied rose strolling ghostly over. Each one with its sunset nova quenched in amber on its headstone. Each of its stopped explosions driven down to juice in some white withering berry there.

# SINCE YOU LEFT

"Since I left you there seems to be so much more between us."
— *in a letter from my ex-wife*

Since you left, there are more mountains between us. More wheat fields and winters. More fried people running out of forests, more frazzled antelopes writhing in pain. Since you left, there are more car accidents between us. I could infect cities with my wonder at your absence and all the roads would curl into question marks and point towards each other in a useless period of pure distilled perplexity. They would put up road signs asking "Why?" And many wise scholars would stand by them all day saying "Because." Because we are obedient. Because we have followed the roads to the ever-present period and are now ending all our months with circular, unanswerable confusions. Because there is a vast ignorance larger than my mouth and I can't get it out of me — I shouldn't be here. I shouldn't exist. I should be half a tiger. A semi-butterfly. I should be a spider without legs, but you are there, and I am here, and like infinity it boggles me. Since you left, astronauts have danced on the moon and there are more footprints between us. More closed doors and sick Indians. More pipelines and Canadians. Big hooting ones with flags and borderlines. I would have to go over many jingoists to get to you. Since you left, several foetal mayors have been aborted on Main Street and there is more semen between us. I am sending you a picture of the doctor at work now on one of our streets trying to remove a suicide from it. He's saying, "He's malignant! He's huge under there — already bloated into sewers and subways." Since you left there are more black doves in oil slicks between us. More levity and false laughter. More orchards and suns and stars. I have made a round ring of helium and send it to you now without regret. Catch it as you would a quoit. One on each appendage. O, I would come to you. I would come to you but everywhere I turn there is this old lady in my way trying to scrub the shadow of a "Z" off the sidewalk. I say, "Hey look, it is just part of the word "Zoo," you know, why not wait for night and begin again in the morning?" But no, she just moves onto the "O's" and throws me a little bit of meat. If I ever get to you, I will have to be jumping and hungry. I will have to be very happy. If I ever get to you at all, it will be like scissors getting to the other edge of paper. Two slices will fall away from everything and with a strange sliced face like a kiss I will say "Hi" and perform several miracles while you're not looking.

## PROPOSAL

You can have my magazine of flesh, my tattooed book, my sick face corrupted by the heart. I'll bring you a bouquet of little angers broken open, my ivory dog's head, my flaccid chairs, my bed of noodles. I'll bring you the burnt apple-black moon, the sick moon of my longing. I have an appetite for you. It is a little black bag with an elephant in it and a pinhead that he jumps on. I have all the quicksilver ever knocked from an apple with an axe. You can have the Hershey cows, the television coats. You can have the great Broadway orange, my crow of talcum, my monkey Madonna shrieking in the moonlight. I will give you nerves and the wool picked from daisies. I will bring you ten cups filled with dew, a table made of peas. You may have the impossible dancers, the giddy, the staggering maple. You may have the poplars drunk, the laughing antelopes. I will bring you ears, ointments, wigs, and jewels — just stay.

# MORE!

More! More! More! Bring down your miraculous mouth over mine and make me green to the throat. Make me plush velvet to the breast. Leave a kiss at the base of me, at the broken axle where the blood spins 'round. Kiss me where you can with hot kisses you have saved up, soaked through your weeping body in nights of longing — kisses caught in you — captured like shoals of struggling fish desperate to get out and melt at my mouth, to be immolated by the heat of having me. Save up for me those kisses I save for you and we will let them, like a horde of crimson warriors, destroy one another. Then we will be locked together — share the same bone of pleasure, the same ache of fulfillment, to ease, afterwards, the soft words out of us, all stored up and unspeakable for so long. And let us keep kissing even then, like animals who have fainted by the water and unconsciously lap there, long past satisfaction, till we are brimming over with each other, aching with intense pleasure.

## POEM FOR A FISHERWOMAN, 1983

On a long holy strand of my finest spit I am fastening a hook to the heavens — a silver hook and a wish made of will. You, my love, are the bait — you and the boy and the family. If they will swallow that, then we just might catch an angel. We just might fly. Otherwise we will climb, fixed to one another by faith and suspicion — man, woman, and child high in the sun — that thin strand stretching beneath us, threatening to break. I am drawing in a golden globe of undying fish, flipping even now in my palm, holy and alive in my lips. Ah sweet love, on a thin green strand of phlegm I am drawing a hospital in — a holy hospital of brutalized angels. Angels who won't do. Big church angels and some commercial angels too. I have caught a bottle of holy glue, the same holy glue that God uses, fastening himself to the religions. Fast holy glue that sets in a second and I am spreading it on the earth for you, hoping for just a touch of paradise, some little soul-bit of me in you to settle down. We will touch, we two. We will embrace, and afterwards, because of it, no matter how thin, our bodies and our souls will always be joined by a little strand. So, babe, wind me in. Take me down off the rooftops. Pull me out of the deep rapids, the highest part of the sky where the cold wind goes by. Draw me in from streets, miles away, by magic. And never cut this strand. Never even try, for there is not one blade, not one twilight, not one sharp mouth deep enough for that. You will always be joined to me now, slender fisherwoman. Just you and Saturn on a string. You and the world hanging from a thread with your heart and your lust and your blood. So draw down heaven, love. Tug that silver string and drag this kite out of the whirlwind. Come, into this gamble, this boat pulled into the unknown — this journey in the wild current.

# TALES OF A DOMESTIC HEART

I turn off the switch to your heart. Your heart goes out, with no glowing. Your heart, your heart. I have a special blinder, a piece of fine lead for your heart. I have a parasol and sunglasses for your heart. A special myopia developed over years of staring — years of squinting into mirrors searching for beauty. Now I can't see your heart. O blow it up, my loved one, swell it up and over till it's everywhere.

Your heart is squeezed into the corner. It is under the bed. Always scurrying from vision. Your fugitive heart. Silent, obvious. Your huge heart, red and sore. Your angry heart, sick of being silent and invisible. Your heart needs a shake-up. If you redo your heart, then, when it is huge and stuck on a chair weeping, perhaps I will see it. Take off the blinders to your heart. Get your heart out of its scared shell. I want to see your heart. Please send me your heart. Let's strip your heart.

When she is angry she throws her heart in the bath. Huge and wooden it just sits there floating, cracking, and splintering. I open the door and say, "Are you all right?" I go over and kiss her heart, burning my lips, forgetting the great heat of her heart. The heart just floats in the bath. I can hear it hissing. Push the heart under — it comes to the surface. I say sorry to her heart. Next, she puts her heart up on a pole in the living room. She walks around looking sullen, doing the dishes. "What's wrong?" I ask her. "Nothing," she answers, but the heart swells and lets out a huge crack on top of the pole. I quietly take the heart down from the pole, open the windows and get sunshine on her heart. She is still in the kitchen doing the dishes. Becoming cruel, I put her heart down with the pots and pans and leave her in there, furiously weeping and scrubbing, the heart still beating in the leftover soup. Finally I take her to bed and curl around her heart. I curl around it like a foetus. I curl around it till it is as big as a boulder and I am like a tiny leech, a tiny worm in her heart. I curl around it under the covers until she comes to bed for it. She slips in beside me, deathly cold, her feet like stones, and then in the darkness I open her ribs and slip it in. It will only work for a while — enough for a little peace to make her warm. I put her heart back in behind her breast and I rub her till it is beating madly. I rub her till her heart is stoked and then when it goes off, I go to sleep. In the morning her heart is breaking through again. She takes it with her to work. She keeps it in a purse, in a bell and some cups. In the morning her heart is small and efficient. It is rolled up in leaves and left for the children, left for the winds and workers till she returns. Her heart. Her beautiful heart.

# DOT AND DASH

A touch of my skin to a touch of hers is added like protoplasmic spice, weird flavours at the edge. And when a finger crosses over and touches a cheek there is a titanic ignition. If we want to become like two sheets of glass smashed together, if we want to be two harps fused in music by a fire-burst, then we must lie in bed and plug in, willing to go up like an entire meadow, a country the size of a field, a bed as small as a river, and float away in flowery silliness. Look and see the large blossoms in the bed then, too big for a room, bent over toward the window and reading poetry together. What I want to do is another experiment — hurl my matter at hers at great speed, setting off a hairy star, another wide-limbed sun-shriek that lets out the dark corners of the room, like a message to the stars each time a tongue touches a tongue.

# DIFFICULT HEAVEN

Difficult heaven — a drop of rain — slides down the window held up only by friction, the buoyancy of earth-air. My beloved has a difficult heaven in her thighs and I am the window holding her up for as long as I can. Soon she will be one with the dew, one with the water running rivulets down houses and streets to streams. Soon she will be one with the ocean, crashing down and flattening out to a long streaming run up a beach. She and I keep afloat a difficult heaven by much heavy breathing, by many big words and miraculous acts. I can hold up the sea on the tip of my tongue. I can pierce through a globe of dew and see a whole world come apart with a groan, everything sliding in its flat wash, wild, up a smooth beach. We are careening jugs, great urns of oil being spilled. We are jewels and barley scattered in the tide where gulls pick at us in a frenzy, gone and gone with our legs kicking up. See how the rippling separates the sunset into a thousand flames? Well we are like that — life flows in and casts our light into days and days, our arms upraised, our bodies tributaries to it — reflections that must dance on the tide awhile before they're drawn back into the lap of time.

# SOMETIMES THERE IS A WAY

I touch my soul to yours at the mouth and two needles knock in our hearts. Self-absorbing colours mix in heat maps — purple and red turning gold, all the colours of creation flashing through us in neon pulses as we writhe. Aaaaah, give me the touch of my lover's hand upon my neck like a brush in paint. Give these colours in my head the touch of spirit her eyes will need. Sometimes there is a way. Get your love to lay you down ten miles long and be a lake in the sunset — a long, thin finger lake, a lake that darkens with pain and mystery in the evening, rising up and menacing the cliffs of love. Let your love then lay upon the stillness at the centre of you, a hand that spreads it, calming you out to a lapping and shimmering in a moonlight that is green. Sometimes there is a way out of human agony, my love. Sometimes we can move with kisses dark rivers of pain in the throat. There are regions of sunrise in my being which can break their boundaries and spread if you but touch the key. O I am here to announce that there definitely is a way, and our bodies, our gestures, are maps to it that we must follow like blind ones touching each curve of Braille in ecstasy as we wander along the blond and tawny roads.

## LOVE AS THOUGH

Your mouth is the first mouth — the mouth I approach from the mountains, from the stars — swooping like a hawk to catch it turning, to catch it white and hot. Ah, breathe down deep into my substance and come away with a memory of the source of things — the river returning on itself with salmon and men. Come down by the falling water in me. Chip off all the old edges of your rigid life and come running again in rocks and waves and winds, till both of us are worn down, eroded to grains of sand, our bodies strewn over a thousand lands, lost in a million winds, on the boots even of the star travelers. Let us unravel mysteries long knotted and entwined on fate's billion-fingered hand, gnarled about us like these winter trees. Come at last, still patient to the poem in her palm — that simple verse: "Live and be happy." From one another grow as though from a mutual soil. As though stones could not keep their shape and the moon depended on it. As though it had all come down to our love. Because it all has come down to our love.